19/09/14

Dear 4/16

CW00520670

PA (D)

BUS

Please renew/return this item by the last date
shown. Please call the number below:

Renewals and enquiries: 0300 123 4049

Textphone for hearing or   0300 123 4041
speech impaired users:

www.hertsdirect.org/librarycatalogue

Hertfordshire

TELL IT TO A STRANGER:
STORIES FROM THE 1940S

Persephone Book N°15
Published by Persephone Books Ltd 2000
Reprinted 2001 and 2011
First published in *Selected Stories* (Maurice Fridberg, 1947) and
The Pick of Today's Short Stories (Odham's Press, 1949)

Endpapers taken from 'Web', a screen-printed rayon crêpe
dress fabric designed by Graham Sutherland for
Cresta Silks in 1947, reproduced by courtesy of the
Trustees of the Victoria & Albert Museum, London.

Typeset in ITC Baskerville by Keystroke,
Wolverhampton

Printed and bound in Germany by
GGP Media GmbH, Poessneck

978 1 903155 042

Persephone Books Ltd
59 Lamb's Conduit Street
London WC1N 3NB
020 7242 9292

www.persephonebooks.co.uk

TELL IT TO A STRANGER:
STORIES FROM THE 1940S
by
ELIZABETH BERRIDGE

🔲🔲🔲🔲🔲🔲🔲

with a new preface by
A.N. WILSON

and a new afterword by
THE AUTHOR

PERSEPHONE BOOKS
LONDON

CONTENTS

◻◻◻◻◻◻◻

PREFACE

A short story with the title 'To Tea with the Colonel' would suggest to many readers that they were about to enter a comfortable and conservative past, an England which was extremely English. Elizabeth Berridge, though, is a true subversive in that you can never guess, when you start to read one of her tales, where it will lead you.

In that particular story, a young woman who has been bombed out of her house in London, and who has sought refuge in the Welsh village where the Colonel resides, finds herself visited by overpowering rage when she enters his big house. (She is only there as a favour to his daughter, who normally gives the old man his tea on the dot of four-thirty, but who on this occasion is unable to do so.) So furious is Miss Morton that she says, 'When I think of the numbers of people your family have kept poor in order to build this house, I want to wreck it all –' But there are two twists, not one, to this quietly disturbing story. First, the old man is deaf, and so he cannot hear what the leftist young Londoner is saying. It inspires her to yet further extremes of rudeness and radicalism. But there is something more poignant to come. He responds to her with such perfect courtesy, that she is stricken with remorse. 'The Colonel would have spoken, but he was no longer in contact with the world. And he had never known what it was to doubt or bitterly regret a cruelty, for he had never been cruel.' He is in fact one of those 'old men who never cheated, never doubted' of whom Betjeman once wrote.

By contrast, in 'Subject for a Sermon', it is the young man coming back from the wars to his Lady Bountiful mother who can upbraid her for her unstinting public spiritedness in the war effort, which leaves him feeling unloved and neglected. He hates his mother – he hates what she and her class and her generation have prepared for him and his age group.

He rails on the women who have called on the men to fight and to make war. 'There were hundreds like you, who called themselves leaders of the nation. . . . They wouldn't try to stop a war, stop their men being killed. No! They wanted to be in on it. Organise it.'

Readers of these beautifully crafted stories will find themselves adjusting a few illusions and preconceptions of the 1939–45 war. They depict a world of shortages, queues for disgusting meat in provincial butchers, homelessness, and anger. Few of the characters are as lucky as the young couple in 'Chance Callers', who find themselves unable to afford accommodation at the end of the war, and who boldly call on a Captain with a big house, hoping for a billet; he leaves them his house and estate in his will. Most Berridge characters bravely struggle on against the odds, maintaining dignity, courage and a sense of life's wonder. Some of these exquisite miniatures are quietly comic – as in 'Woman about the House', a bitterly rueful tale about a man who is left by his wife in fairly harsh circumstances and who finds himself, at the end, smiling in his sleep. Others have not merely a terribleness, but an almost supernatural terribleness: read 'Lullaby' – so short, so painful.

So much which concerns the publishing and promoting of English fiction seems to be a matter of chance. Why are some unimpressive writers so famous, and some good ones so unjustly neglected? Elizabeth Berridge is quite easily as impressive as many of the more famous names of the twentieth century, and her band of devoted readers and admirers will rejoice at the republication of these stories which will surely increase her readership.

She is a novelist of distinction who is also – and this is a rarity – equally at home in the quite different medium of the short story, with its need for an iron discipline and control. Many of the masters of this genre, carried away by their cleverness, their ability to encapsulate much in a little room, either convey or actually possess the quality of heartlessness: one thinks of Guy de Maupassant or Somerset Maugham. Others – and one thinks primarily of Chekhov – are able to retain the discipline of the medium but suffuse its tight confines with warmth. This is the quality of Elizabeth Berridge's stories which sends us back to them, which makes us read and re-read until they have become friends. The woman who has lost her baby – and the female doctor; the house-proud men and women who have lost their possessions through acts of war, people coming to terms with bereavement: they are all seen with the eyes not only of penetration and profound artistic intelligence, but also with gentleness and love. These stories are much more than period pieces. They have robustly stood the test of half a century and are as freshly impressive as when they first delighted an earlier generation of readers in those very dark days which they describe.

A.N. Wilson
London, 2000

TELL IT TO A STRANGER:
STORIES FROM THE 1940S

SNOWSTORM

▢▢▢▢▢▢▢

The doctor watched the green charabanc emerge from among the yews flanking the drive and draw up in front of the wide stone porch.

They were late. From habit she glanced at her watch. That meant she would be late examining them. As she looked the door of the charabanc opened and the women dropped heavily one by one, on to the snow-buried gravel. For a moment she was reminded of the blundering honey-bees of summer, over-weighted with pollen. But the image passed as they clustered together before the house, gazing about, their faces cold, movements distrustful. Swiftly she counted them. Two missing. That always happened: a husband or mother insisting on the child being born at home, raid or no raid. Turning from the window she caught a glimpse of a scarlet coat. Startled by the colour, she looked closer. She saw a girl standing apart, as if in denial, and something about the arrogant head with its swathes of rich hair disturbed her. The others would be no trouble, but – with a definite feeling of unrest the doctor drew back into the room as Sister Matthews stepped out from the porch to welcome them.

The women looked hardly more at ease when they gathered for their examination. The doctor glanced swiftly at them as the nurse set up the screens at the far end of the room. They looked strange and pathetic, most of them in their early twenties, schoolgirl faces peaked with cold and the unaccustomed surroundings. They seemed unable to believe that the journey was over: the cold journey started early that morning from among unfamiliar streets, bombed buildings looking like half-destroyed snow-castles; the long journey during which each had time to realise that before she could return there would be pain and a new experience, to be borne alone. And at last the flat, frost-bitten country, which bewildered even the driver, had yielded them up to shelter – no, they could not quite believe it.

It seemed to the doctor that pregnancy had given back to each of them an innocence which sat hauntingly behind her eyes. It mixed with the flame of fear that gathered up and exposed each separate strand of emotion, weighing more finely the balance between reason and hysteria. She felt this fear reach out to claim her as she started the examinations, and bending over each full-formed belly, placed so incongruously above a girl's slender legs, she felt the full flood of power take possession of her hands, giving out calmness and strength, guiding her to the living child. Confidence was the first essential. Something had to replace the loss of home, the cosseting of friends. Here you made the first move towards a successful delivery.

She was fully absorbed when the girl she had seen from the window walked round the screen. She recognised her by the thick hair and upright carriage. The doctor saw her eyes were large, the pupils dilated, dark with green lights. It was as if she continually strained to focus attention away from her heavy body. She sat on the couch and drew away from the nurse's hands, pulling off her clothes. The doctor felt her shock of interest deepen and realised for the first time that Sister Matthew's actions were repellent – impersonal as a brothel-keeper's, partially undressing a girl for a client's appraisal. 'That will do, Sister,' she said, and the tone of her voice made the nurse withdraw, hurt, to the table, where she made a show of checking names.

What lay behind those painfully wide eyes? wondered the doctor as she carried on the examination. 'Relax,' she said. 'Relax.' But the girl's muscles seemed locked. That would mean trouble later. 'Relax,' she said again, 'You must let yourself go loose. There's nothing to be afraid of. I won't hurt you.'

That touched something in the still face and a flare of colour covered the cheeks. 'I'm not afraid,' said the girl, 'this is just a process, like anything else . . .' but she relaxed and smiled slightly. The doctor nodded approval.

'That's better,' she said. What a voice the girl had. After the hesitancy of the others, their frayed enunciation, its clearness was astounding. It was like her own voice, decisive, entirely under control. Sister Matthews handed her a slip of paper and frowned slightly, motioning the girl to dress. 'We'll be keeping you in here for a few days,' she said, 'then we'll see about billeting you out.'

The girl sat up and pulled on her clothes. 'Oh?' she said, 'I expected that. My blood-pressure's always been erratic.' She laughed, as if here she was on the doctor's ground and could claim equality. The doctor looked at her sharply.

'Then you'll know how to take care of yourself, no smoking, no alcohol.'

'Alcohol? In this wilderness?' the girl raised her eyebrows. 'All right to go now?' she asked.

'Lady touch-me-not,' murmured the sister as she readjusted the screens. She was angry and her eyes were unkind. 'She'll soon find her level here.'

* * *

In the days that followed the doctor and each one of the staff saw Theresa Jenkins moving silently among the other women, accepting no mien of behaviour. Hers was a dark dress where the others wore flowered smocks, full, but not full enough to disguise the bouncing burdens which governed their every movement. She walked erect and lightly in contrast to the lurching tread of those around her. She did not knit or sew to patterns, she very seldom read. But every day she walked the two miles into the nearest market town and brought back silks or wool or books for the others.

It was here the doctor next encountered her; on a day of blizzard when the snow drove horizontally across the heath, lying flat as a footprint between the Hall and Airton. She was leaning against the low wall on the bridge, the wind whipping the scarlet coat around her. Below, the waterfall was frozen. She did not look round when the car drew up until the doctor's voice, sharp with command, came through the blinding flakes. The door was opened and she climbed in, shutting it behind her with dead fingers. 'A little exercise I said, not a cross-country run.' Firmly the doctor's fingers rubbed the windscreen and adjusted the wipers. They moved forward as a camouflaged Army lorry passed them in a white cloud.

'Yes, it was a bit much today,' said the girl; she was blue round the lips. 'But I'm well ballasted.'

'Well, I'm putting you and your ballast to bed when we get back, and you're staying there.'

Theresa looked coolly at the determined face beside her and shrugged. 'But not in one of those great communal bedrooms – there's no fire, and the beds are awful, filled with chicken-food . . .'

They entered the drive. There was a tense, sparring atmosphere between them. The doctor fell back on her power of position. She said: 'I'm putting you into solitary confinement. You're in for an attack of 'flu.'

As she drove the car round to the back of the house she thought: She upsets me, makes me feel – Oh, I don't know.

* * *

In the nursery on the ground floor there was never complete silence. Nurse Griffith, standing by the weighing machine, looked with sudden exasperation along the rows of baskets. From nearly each one came a thin gasping cry or a long effortless wail. 'If they'd only stop. Just for a moment. All together,' she said aloud. But as if in defiance a quacking gurgle joined in. 'Well, you'll be gone tomorrow, glory be,' she observed, 'and I wish your mother joy of you.'

The door opened and two other nurses came in, carrying bundles under their arms, bundles done up in striped blankets and shaped like paper twists for sweets.

'Bullying them again, Griffith?' said one of them, and laying one of her burdens in a basket she sat down and unwrapped the other, revealing a tiny crumpled face and one red fist. She started to change its napkin.

'I was just telling Donald Duck how glad I shall be when he goes.'

'Poor little Donald, I shall miss him. Such an *individualist*,' said the other nurse. Her eyes were dark and moist. She looked as if she overflowed with love for each baby there.

Nurse Griffith grunted. She was Scotch and spared her emotion. 'Have you seen Doctor Meredith?' she inquired, 'I want her to look at young Rolly – he'll have to be circumcised, I think.'

'She's due any minute.' The dark-eyed nurse was frowning at the child she had unwrapped and who now lay screaming on the scales. She checked the weight, then whisked the child off. 'Not enough food. I thought her milk was going off. Come along, chicken.' She took up a bottle warming by the fire and settled herself in a chair. The child's face uncrumpled as its mouth found the teat. 'I can give a guess where she is though. In Ward 12, and there's nothing wrong with Mrs. Jenkins now.'

'Nothing apart from having a baby,' said Nurse Griffith. Her face was hard and dour. 'I said to her the other day: soon be over, Mrs. Jenkins. Next week for you. And she gave me such a look. Sat up and said: no doubt you're looking forward to it. Well, I'm not. So I said one baby more or less makes no difference to me, my girl. I've brought enough into the world.'

'Doctor seems to get on well with her, though,' said the other nurse.

'Get on well!' Nurse Griffith sniffed. 'There *was* an atmosphere when I went in this morning. Cut it with a knife, you could.' She broke off as the door opened and the doctor came in with the matron, who was in her out-door clothes. She was frowning slightly, and Nurse Griffith looked keenly at her. It seemed that the wailing of the babies affected her more than usual this morning, her frown had deepened as they walked down the rows together. Carefully she asked questions and conducted examinations in her usual capable manner, but it seemed to the nurse that her eyes were preoccupied.

'You're quite right, nurse,' she said, 'Baby Rolly needs to be circumcised. I'll see his mother.' Turning to the matron she said: 'I think I'll leave those vaccinations now, and do all three together later.' With a nod she left them and walked quickly from the nursery.

'Perhaps she's a little tired,' said the matron, 'she *does* work hard.'

But the doctor was not feeling tired as she walked across the cold stone hall and down the passage opposite to where the narrow wooden stairs ran up from just past the dining-room door. As she went slowly up to the next floor and passed along the narrow corridor of closed doors she thought, a little shakily, that was a strange thing for a patient to say to me, it's never happened before. She had passed through the width of the house and now stood on the first main landing. The huge polished space of floor with the broad and shining staircase curving down to the hall below and up to the labour ward on the next floor quietened her. As always its familiarity was startling; she might have been born here. The wide windows framed the winter and for a moment she stopped, undecided. She's no right to speak to me like that, she thought, and made to go to her own room, with the comforting china procession along the mantelpiece; ducks, elephants, donkeys – but the pricking unease forbade her the comfort of a fire or even the absorption of study. No right?

She had said, going into Ward 12 that morning, 'You'll be having your baby very soon, Mrs. Jenkins. I like to tell the more intelligent mothers exactly what happens, it makes it easier . . .' but she had been unable to go on, seeing the irony on the other's face. The girl sat there in bed, a little flushed, the eyes mocking her, openly mocking the whole procedure of birth; the diet, the routine, the urine tests.

'I expect I shall find out for myself, thanks,' she said. Her voice was casual as if she were turning away an itinerant salesman. The doctor went white, but forced herself to say, as if she had heard nothing: 'And if there's anything worrying you, preventing you from sleeping, you'll tell me, won't you? It's important not to have anything on your mind.' She turned from the bed and walked over to the fireplace as she spoke, and standing in the attitude of her father, with legs apart and hands clasped loosely, she felt some of his strength flow into her.

'Yes, people seem to hate you having anything on your mind,' came the voice from the bed. 'Calm motherhood, that's the idea, isn't it? The most beautiful time of a woman's life, preparing for the little stranger – ' her whole face twisted suddenly, but whether with pain or disgust the doctor could not make out.

'That wasn't my idea at all,' she said. 'Some people think that way, others don't. Nurse Barnes tells me you're not sleeping. I want to know why.' She had accepted the challenge flung out by the mocking face, but immediately regretted it. For the girl had sent her a glance meaning: is it really your business? The door opened then and Nurse Griffith had come in.

Now, standing in the faint chilled sunlight, she thought. Of course it's my business. Did the girl think that having a baby was as easy as that? Did she think that at such a time she could remain private and apart? Where would you be in medicine without method and routine? I won't let her bother me, she thought, and shrugging, turned to go up the stairs past the labour ward. I must see Mrs. Rolly.

The visit to the quiet ward with its rows of docile women knitting or talking was curiously soothing. Here was her defence, among the soft-eyed women, soft as if milk flowed through every vein. No complications. No questioning of her authority and importance. They were gentle as cattle in good pasture. I must go back to Ireland, she thought as she left the ward in a small stir behind her. That's what's wrong. I need a holiday. Whenever things were too difficult – examinations near, her mind caught at the low green image of the land near her home.

She looked in at the dispensary on her way down.

'Oh, Nurse Barnes,' she said, 'give Mrs. Jenkins a sleeping draught tonight.'

From below, distantly came the blanketed ring of the telephone. 'I'll go,' she said, 'matron's out.' But as she ran down the main staircase the bell stopped abruptly. Opening the door of the matron's sitting room she saw Theresa Jenkins at the desk, a blue dressing-gown clasped round her, and holding the receiver tightly to her ear.

The girl looked up.

'Long distance,' she said, her hand over the mouthpiece, 'For me.'

She looked so composed, so *right*, sitting there in the matron's room, at the matron's desk that the doctor's irritation concerning her flamed into rage and hatred. She let her feelings out in a sentence she knew with all her being would hurt. 'You know you women are not allowed in here,' she said, leaning deliberately against the door, eyebrows raised. She saw the deep flush spread over the girl's face, and knew she had scored. But next moment the girl was speaking into the phone. Her voice was hurried, a little shaken. 'Hullo, yes darling, it's me.' The doctor could hear nothing of the voice at the other end of the line, but it spoke at length and the girl listened, her colour ebbing to normal. Then, 'Of course,' she said.

The doctor walked towards the wide white fireplace where the matron's cat, grey as the ash falling from the logs, arched itself for a caress. What can I say to her, she thought, automatically smoothing the quick ears. The quiet of the pale walls, the cat's electric purring, the soft private answers of the girl at the telephone helped the doctor to define the feelings which had disturbed her since that first glimpse of the scarlet coat through the window. Odd how she had felt there would be trouble from her. She was always right in these things. She remembered the old man who had said he could see the power about her: 'You could heal by a touch, dear young lady,' and the sweat was ridged above his eyebrows, caught in the bushiness of them. He had died the next day. Shaking herself free of that Dublin slum she looked into the fire. The girl was different, outside her power. It was like being faced by a new and hostile world. She heard footsteps and laughter go past the door and felt again the tremendous difference between the girl at the desk and those others. They had accepted life in the hospital as a logical conclusion to the months of carrying the child; putting behind them their private lives. At this time everything was swamped in the expectation of birth; husbands were unreal, the newspapers not important. They were the childbearers.

The doctor pushed a log in place with her foot and watched the sudden sparks showering. The cat jumped a little. That attitude makes it much easier for us, she thought. Biological, impersonal. The nurses must feel the same.

The girl at the desk was speaking now, purposefully, with a hint of impatience.

She mightn't be having a child at all, thought the doctor with indignation. She goes on exactly as if she were at home, or on a visit. Perhaps her own life is too exciting. As this thought passed through her mind a sudden envy attacked her. It came as unexpectedly as the sound of the clock outside the door, striking with the ponderous hesitation of old age.

Snaking over the countryside went the wire connecting Theresa's life with Rowley Hall. Somewhere out in the snow, in a city, a man was sitting, or maybe standing, one leg up on a chair, watching his cigarette spiral in smoke as he spoke into the receiver. Other worlds, other relationships. The whole organisation of Rowley Hall meaning nothing beside them. She, the doctor, of as little significance as an obliging bus-conductor, a helpful policeman. She felt enclosed in this smooth-running house, its babies across the hall, its mothers above. Yet they all depended on her. The thought brought no pride, only a sense of suffocation and a sudden *I would give it all up for a telephone call from a city* . . .

The receiver was hung up with a small metallic noise.

For a moment both women stared at it. The line was dead now and the snow-wastes lay impassible.

'Come and get warm before you go upstairs,' said the doctor, and the girl moved slowly, heavily towards the fireplace. Her face was like stone.

'Cats are so magnificently selfish,' she said, staring down.

The doctor knew it was her moment; the girl looked drained, as if contact with the vital world outside had been too much for her. She was lost between the two existences; a word and she would be shattered. As a woman, cunning, before the fire, the doctor could spin a web of words – she could capture that world, suck it from the girl. But she said: 'I'll walk upstairs with you' and put a hand on her elbow. 'You'd better get into bed and rest.' Without a word they left the room and went up the shallow stairs in silence. Something has happened, thought the doctor. I do hope . . . but her fear was a vague thing, scarcely yet known to her intuition.

As they turned in to Ward 12 the girl said: 'Matron knew I was expecting a call.' She sat on the bed and knocked off her blue slippers. As she settled against the pillows the doctor pulled the clothes round her. She felt at ease doing these things, her brain working: does she need sal volatile, a cup of tea? A glance at her watch told her tea would be brought round within ten minutes. She sat down.

'Do you really want your baby?' she asked.

They looked at each other. The distance between them was so vast, so wearying, that it had to be accepted, could never be crossed.

'You'd like me to want it, wouldn't you?' said Theresa, exhaustion seemed to edge her voice, and increase the hidden store of rancour. Or was it bitterness, torment, sorrow? 'You'd like to feel it meant everything to me, and I was relying on you to get me through.'

'What nonsense,' said the doctor. Despite her reason she felt suddenly malicious. 'You're just one patient, and I don't want any trouble. You're the sort of person to cause it . . .'

'Trouble?' Theresa laughed outright. 'No, you're not used to that, are you? The only people you can deal with are weaklings – the world's temporary throw-outs. The world's too sharp a place for you . . .'

The doctor was stung to anger. So she thought that being a doctor was a hide-out! There was exaltation in her hatred as she replied: 'And you,' she said, 'And you? What do you do to face the world – what do you do for it?'

But the girl turned away; her face suddenly dulled.

'I?' she asked, and dropped her hand on the sheet. 'I?' Glancing at the doctor, still white and taut by the fire, she smiled, almost kindly. 'I am the pincushion you sit on by mistake, or perhaps a rash between the shoulderblades you cannot reach. A very special function. And very necessary. Look how it has roused you.'

The doctor turned away with a gesture. Lack of sleep, nerves. She didn't like it. Futile to waste the energy of anger on her.

The door opened and a nurse brought in the tea.

'Mrs. Stimpson is up in the labour ward, doctor,' she said, placing the tray in front of the girl in bed, on to her flattened knees. 'Run it pretty close.' And she moved over to the windows and hauled the blackout into position. 'Went into town this afternoon to have her hair set. What will they do next?'

'I'll go up,' said the doctor. As she went from the room she saw a letter lying on the tray. 'I was expecting this,' she heard Theresa say to the nurse, and as she walked away up the corridor it was as if some other world had brushed against her own, brushed past and was gone forever.

* * *

The next afternoon Mrs. Stimpson lay in the smaller post-natal ward, which was on the ground floor next to the nursery. Centuries back it had been a refectory, built on to the side of the house with its own fine pointed roof, all timber. Later, as sunroom, the roof had been cut off and sheets of glass laid across, so that now, lying flat in bed and gazing up, it was as if the sky itself domed the room.

Red Cross nurses stood on chairs pulling on the cords operating a complicated system of blackout.

'Goodbye to the evening star,' said one of them as the black canvas was slowly manoeuvred across the darkening sky. Mrs. Stimpson glanced at the empty bed beside her.

'Still worrying, Stimmy?' said the woman in the bed opposite. 'She'll be all right, you'll see.' She broke off as one of the regular nurses entered the ward. 'Any news, nurse?'

'Doctor's still up there. She looks worn out.' The little nurse, trim and young, was concerned. 'Mrs. Jenkins will be down some time this evening . . .'

'Boy or girl?' asked the woman eagerly.

The nurse turned away. They would know later.

'She lost it. A boy,' she said, and to calm the sudden gasp quickly went on, 'Now, Sister will be round in a minute. What shall it be? Liquid paraffin or cascara?'

Mrs. Stimpson lay still. She remembered the hurry and shock of the matron, brought at midnight to the labour ward; the quiet sobs of pain, the sudden high note in the doctor's voice. Then silence and they had quickly carried her down here.

There was another empty bed in the ward, and the occupant was moving uncertainly about. The floor seemed ominous as a stage, an empty dance floor; too big, too shiny to cross. Enviously the others watched her. Already she was apart from them. They had seen her dressing, shared the pleasure in pulling on the narrow elastic belt, the slim skirt. With the putting on of normal clothes she had stepped out of the circle of their small world. She became once more the wife, the mother with a home of her own. In a day or two she would be gone, in a week forgotten: they would never meet again. She moved across to put more coal on the fire, then sat down, grave. Fancy losing your baby, she thought, shocked. Tomorrow at nine she was to bath hers. In a month, in a week, it would be a common thing, but now it was terrifying. The experience upstairs would be forgotten too, forgotten as were all shattering things: the edge off them, anybody's adventure.

The woman by the fire stirred, shivered a little. She must get back to bed.

Later, when the whole ward was settled into sleep, the firelight tossing darkness into corners, a nightnurse pushed open the door. She wore a thick black cape against the chill of the stone corridors, and carried a storm lantern held high. Four figures came heavily into the room, bearing a stretcher. Silently they opened the bed next to Mrs. Stimpson and slid their burden into it. After a careful survey they went out again, four shadows following them to the door. There was no sound from the bed.

Once outside the matron put her arm round the doctor's shoulders. 'You did all you could, my dear. You were wonderful,' she said, 'it was not your fault. Not in the least. The girl – ' she let her hand fall. Hopeless, disgraceful.

'It's the first baby I've lost,' said the doctor, 'it's never happened before. To lose a life – ' she shook her head.

'*You* didn't lose it,' said the matron sharply. 'I can't understand it. Such a dreadful thing to do – we must ask her – so wicked – wicked . . .'

'No, she must sleep now,' said the doctor. 'Must give her time.' Time. She was dazed with the strain and shock. Her mind was empty and yet terribly clear. I couldn't have saved the child. She saw to that. Too late . . .

The matron opened her sitting-room door. 'A cup of tea,' she said, 'before you go to bed.'

They sat down before the fire and the matron made tea. The doctor carefully built up the dying fire. The exactitude soothed her hands, she felt steadied. She could bring her mind round to face the thought that had been tugging at her all day, ever since the bitter knowledge of what the girl had done was clear to her. Theresa had known what she was going to do – perhaps she had discussed it over the phone, with the doctor in the room. But that was too horrible. Perhaps it was the letter. Or, worst of all, she may have done it knowing what a shattering effect it would have on her.

In defence against the evil she felt beating at the walls of her house, the doctor said aloud: 'Every child we bring into the world is some sort of victory. We must always be against the destroyers.'

The matron poured milk into the cups and tested the tea. Her face, smooth as a nun's, looked towards the other woman with her young blond head and the blue ribbon threading the hair. How young she looks, she thought. Yet I suppose she's right. I suppose that's what a hospital is for. And yet was it? To her a hospital entailed lists of necessities, changing faces, great quietness and clean smells. When I was young, she thought. But years pass and peaks become plains; the war against disease and germs becomes a routine thing. You win and you lose and miracles sometimes happen. I am old, she thought. I fight in my own way.

She shook her head.

'The risk,' she said in awe. 'What a risk to take, and how wicked! Yes, wicked after all these months – ' For an instant she knew grief at the thought of the flawless kicking child, a sound boy. Life in the shell-frail fingers and curled toes. To cut this life off, which was the world's life, belonged to the world – how? – with that fall downstairs? Wicked, wicked. Denying God a life. She shook this thought away, cast away too, the little cold curled body in the white wrappings. It would have to be buried . . .

'Your tea, my dear,' she said, 'I'll have to take you in hand, I can see. Can't have our doctor cracking up.'

In her own room later, the doctor remembered this phrase. Our doctor. It set the tempo of her dreams. Theresa at the end of a narrow corridor, a naked child held high, always eluding her. Theresa laughing, big-bellied; calling in the soundless medium of a dream-shout: Doctor! Our doctor! And near dawn, a procession of women passing, herself in a cage, and each woman having a key to fasten the many locks. Our doctor, said their devoted faces. Dear doctor.

All the next day Theresa slept. She had a pale, burnt-out look to her, and her mouth lay defenceless and innocent. What sort of woman is she? thought the doctor, what sort of life has she? Is she really married? What will she do? The doctor stood over her, thinking, probing. But the sleeping face was closed to her.

As she left the ward, she saw the dark look in Nurse Griffith's eyes and on an impulse took her aside and said what was in her own mind, said it as much in warning to herself. 'We are here to get people well, nurse. Their lives outside are not our concern; we are not judges. I don't want the other women to hear about this. She lost her baby, that is all. And she is to be treated exactly as they are.' Looking into the hard Scotch face she knew the ways an unpopular patient could be treated. A rough shouldering whilst making the bed or changing dressings, delay with the bedpan, pillows set uncomfortably. A dozen small unkindnesses. 'Very well, doctor,' said the nurse stiffly.

It helped the doctor to give these instructions. It gave her ascendancy over that other world, sensed through a phone call, seen in a letter, but strangely missing from the relaxed face on the pillow. All that day she was at peace. She was taking no advantages, the two worlds lay quiescent.

The next morning she watched the girl wake up, turning on her back, the eyes suddenly wide and dark. Her arms were bent up from the elbows and the palms of her hands lay on the pillow either side of her face. 'Philip,' she said.

The doctor was moving forward to lay her hand on the girl's forehead, but the voice, so weak and certain, made her draw back sharply. Philip? so that was the man. Her husband? The action attracted the girl's gaze and in an instant she understood. 'Could I have something to drink?' she asked.

19

* * *

In the days that followed she gradually recovered. Silently she sat propped high and watched the other women as they knitted or talked or fed their children. At first they did these things almost furtively, feeling guilt in her quiet presence, but as the days passed they came to expect her silence and almost forgot her. If the peace of the room, with its six low oaken beds and warm mauve blankets flowed into her, she never showed it, although her face softened as her split body healed, and her eyes assumed an abiding sorrow, something indefinable which would never leave them.

One day, early on, at feeding time, the doctor was helping the woman in the next bed when Nurse Griffith dropped a glass and rubber instrument on to the girl's bed. 'You'll need this, Mrs. Jenkins,' she said as she passed on, 'I'll come back and show you how to use it.'

The girl and the doctor looked at it together. 'It's a breast pump,' said the doctor, her hand on the other woman's shoulder. 'You must relax your shoulders,' she said.

Theresa stared at it, then round at the others, busy with their children, each sunk into a cocoon of warm flowing milk.

'Let me show you,' said Nurse Griffith, 'over here. So. Then pump gently here. It's quite easy.'

She went away after a minute and the girl watched the tiny sprays of milk jetting into the glass bowl. Glancing across at the doctor she gave a short laugh. The doctor's fingers trembled. She knew what it meant: the final gesture. But from somewhere deep in her mind echoed the calm voice, the beloved voice: *don't choose medicine unless you believe in it . . .* What did it say, what had he said, all those buried years ago? *People are lost, all of them. Lost in soul or body, mind or spirit, call it what you will. You can help them. You're a healer. I know and you know. Help, heal . . .*

Help, who was to help whom? It was all lies, the voice from the past, your hands' cunning, lies to get you into a bright little, tight little hygienic cage, rubber-sprung – and still you helped nobody.

'Oh doctor,' said the woman beneath her hand. 'Oh doctor,' she said in pain.

The day Theresa Jenkins left Rowley Hall it was snowing again. Flakes hesitated in the still air, settling chill and furtive on windowsills, gravel and in the furrows of the ploughed field before the house.

The doctor saw her as she came across from the stairs, a notice in her hand to pin to the board. Healed, departing, life in the ward behind her, the girl stood in the grey hall, thin and empty-armed. On impulse the doctor went up to her.

'Don't you want to see where your baby – ?'

Theresa looked at her, her lips were reddened for the journey. 'No,' she said. 'Thank you for seeing to all that.'

A car came up the drive, churning through the snow. Theresa picked up her case and held out her hand.

'Good bye,' she said, and the snow blew in as she opened the door.

As the car slowly turned and brushed its way past the overladen yews, the doctor ran to the porch, leaning into the snow and fighting an almost uncontrollable urge to run after it. Suddenly she could not bear to see her go, knowing nothing. It was as if the girl was driving into a void, travelling always out from the place where the child lay, a cold body, never to uncurl. As if with her, she took the whole meaning of the doctor's life, her work. I can't stay here, she thought, moving back to the board in the hall. She tore down the old notice and crumpled it in one swift movement. Have to get another job. Get out in the world. Do something. But what? She looked at her hands; they had made her a doctor. Healer's hands. But what was a doctor? An attendant upon life only. Apart from the main stream: receiving and sending forth, healing and bringing forth. But why? Where did they all go, the healed in body? Looking at her hands, she thought with panic: If I was asked to deliver a child now, what would I do? What do you do? The printed page of one of her text-books was before her. She saw clearly the form of the printed page, the paragraphs, sub-headings. The diagrams, carefully coloured. But the meaning was lost to her, the type meaningless. A nurse crossed the hall and disappeared into the nursery, two babies tucked under her arms. She smiled at the doctor. I must have some reason for staying here in the cold, she thought with a start. Then saw the notice she had to pin up. 'Permission must be obtained . . .' she smoothed it out, and pinned it in a good light. When it was done another surge of irritation ran through her. Nurses and wards, patients and deliveries, was there no end to them? What of the free, the open life outside where you could be a woman, nothing more? Theresa Jenkins had no struggle there – her only problem was to be a woman, how to get through that way.

A doctor had one path to follow; everything must be seen in that one clear light, no muddleheads, no sidetracks, no envy. After all, in medicine you knew too much, perhaps that kept you apart. The earth was teeming, all you did was to direct the flow. We're all the same, she thought; bus-conductors, commissionaires, doctors. She laughed a little. But do they really trust us? How little we know of people, she thought. She shivered, the door was open again.

She had not heard the charabanc churning up the drive, had missed the pull of brakes, and the women dropping heavy as honey-bees to the white-felted ground. Sister Matthews had come through the hall and was gathering the women together, driving them in from the cold.

A touch, like a summons, fell on her arm.

'You're the doctor, aren't you?' said a small cockney voice. The doctor looked round, saw the customary fear, the pinched mouth, hair damp with melting snow. 'My friend, Mrs. Stimpson, told me about you. She said to tell you the baby's doing well, thanks to you. She said you'd take care of me. It's my first – ' the woman paused. Woman? she was little more than a girl. 'A child's a precious thing,' she said shyly.

The doctor was still staring at her. 'Yes,' she said, 'yes, I'm the doctor.' Although the world can turn up and around like the snowstorm in the glass ball, it will settle, and I am still the doctor. She passed a hand over her eyes, as if to wipe away a lifetime's doubt, a six-week torment.

'Don't worry,' she said, 'I'll see you through.'

THE BARE TREE

The grandmother sat in the sun. It was the only thing free of her daughter's influence. I didn't really want to come, she was thinking. I don't like the country – I don't like Pauline. She could say it to herself, secretly, being old; now that Pauline was married, had a son. Now it could not affect her treatment of her daughter.

Shading her eyes, she thought: I hope my sight is not failing, I hope not. That apple blossom is very pretty. But over so soon. Heavy now and over so soon. When you were old, you saw further than the spring of the year; in one pink opening of a bud there was fruitfulness and decay. Looking at the apple tree with its low unpruned branches, she saw the flowers fade and die, small apples form, grow big and lie in baskets; saw the solemn dropping of leaves, the bare tree.

Pauline will be old soon. What will she be like then? A shadow blocked the tree from her. Almost slyly she looked up; if it was her daughter she would pretend to be asleep.

'Ah, Dennis,' she said with pleasure, 'come and sit by me.' It was her grandson; he sat by her side.

'Where are they?' he asked.

'Who? Oh, your father and mother. I expect they have gone down to the village. Do you want them?'

'Not exactly,' said the boy, and looking up, their eyes met, turned away and met again. They laughed.

'You know, Dennis,' said the old lady, turning her face to his, 'I think you are like *our* family.'

'How do you mean, Gran?' He was nineteen and puzzled.

'Oh, never mind,' she said. 'Are you enjoying your holidays?' He lounged beside her and stroked the grass.

'Oh – yes,' he said. 'I rather wanted to go to the Mathers, though. We were planning a walking tour.'

'Then why didn't you?' His grandmother's voice was purposefully astonished. She had learnt how to act. The years had taught her something after all: she was a sly old woman. She smiled; it gave her strength to know this, gave her strength as the sun did, seeping through into dry old bones beneath the soft satin dress.

'He was called up.'

'Called up? Good gracious.' Yes, good gracious. Young Mathers, Tommy, they used to call him, before he went with Dennis to Oxford. Her sight was better then, she could see his face plainly. A ridiculous face with those huge ears.

'He's going into the Air Force.' Dennis's voice was sullen. 'He tossed for it.'

Young Tommy tossing for it. He always did that. Tossed for first in at cricket, tossed for the window seat in a bus.

'What about you, Dennis?' she asked.

'Won't be long now,' he said. 'You'll be getting your papers, too, Gran. Better look out.' Then he laughed, and she knew by the way it rang that his mother was coming through the trees towards them.

Yes, there she was, standing against apple blossom in her pink linen dress. Was it a coincidence? You could never tell with Pauline.

'Lunch!' she sang now across the green distance. 'Lu-unch!'

Dennis jumped up, offered his hand. He was suddenly on edge.

Pauline is still very good looking, thought the old lady, going slowly in on his arm. I wonder why I never liked her. Even as a child her eyes were hard. She challenged me from the cradle.

They found Dennis's parents already at table. Aubrey was carving cold ham with his usual slight hesitancy, the supple sculptor's hands moving delicately with knife and fork.

'Salad, mother?' Pauline's voice was soft. I used to speak to her like that, thought the old lady.

'No, thank you, dear,' she said.

'Oh, just a little, mother! Tomato? Spring onions? You know you love them.'

The old lady passed her plate. 'Just a few,' she said, knowing the smile that would pass between the ends of the table.

'Disgraceful, young Mathers going into the R.A.F.,' said Aubrey suddenly. 'Thought he'd have had more sense – should I say, more integrity.' He was eating his ham testily, his face the sort he moulded himself; thumbed cavities for eyes, a nose like a rock, cheekbones bare and tired with his pursuit of the unattainable.

'What do you mean, father?' Dennis's voice was hostile. 'It's the best of the services.'

'Just listen to him!' His mother's laugh was high. 'As if that were any excuse. He swore last holidays he was a pacifist.'

'That was last year,' said Dennis, flushing. 'The war hadn't really started then. No one can be a pacifist now.'

'What about us?' asked his mother.

She's getting dangerous, thought the old lady, chewing her tomato. Careful, Dennis.

'Oh, well . . .' he spoke lamely. 'That's different. You've been through one war. You know all about it. This one is ours, we've got to learn first hand. Time to be disillusioned afterwards.'

'Rubbish and nonsense!' cried his father. Something was wrong here, something he couldn't correct or scrap and start over again; this was flesh and blood. 'This war is the same as the last. Only this time machines need the men – use them up quicker than spare parts. That's all they want you for, as a spare part.' They wanted me last time, came the bitter remembrance. *Put on that uniform.* The awful silence of the cells, the warders' obscenities. Yet he knew he wanted his son to suffer the same. Wanted to see him stand alone, not go through life sniffing and calling: *We are of the same blood, thou and I.* '. . . But I've said all this before, thought you understood.'

His disgust, his sick despair, made him want to sob, but he spoke once more. 'This war will end the same way, we'll have the same sort of peace, maybe tied up with more red in the red, white and blue. God, you make me sick. After all the

training, the life we've given you . . . ' If his son were a statue
– boy sitting – he would have thrown him down. Instead he
bowed his head to the plate before him. There's only Pauline
now, and she's a woman.

And being a woman, with a woman's terrible flattening
tact, she was glancing at her mother, at her son, saying,
'Hush, Aubrey, he's only a boy,' saying, 'Mother, another
potato?'

The old lady shook her head. That's the way it goes,
from generation to generation, she was thinking. The young
setting up new values which are old as the sun, kicking away
from the parents as a child kicks from the womb. She listened
to the angry, disjointed talk and remembered Pauline at
eighteen. Yes, she had forced her into a bank. She had only
wanted security for her. Only that. Old letters, interviews,
strings being pulled; these things danced through the doors of
her mind, doors kept shut when life was joyous and the eyes
far-seeing. Now with their dimming came the treacherous
beckoning of memory. I was right then, she thought, but now
I know that the young must find their own way. When you
are old, blood-ties are nothing. She laughed a little and her
plate was taken away. She sensed Pauline's glance, the raised
eyebrow, but would say nothing to her.

There was nothing to say, they were just two women now,
and as such could choose whether to speak or be silent with
each other. There could be no more 'mother' and 'daughter',
that was in the past, now they were separate beings. Still,
the bank was a good idea. Tenaciously she clung on to this
thought. Security, a pension, that was something in those

days. After all, she might not have married. Not every girl marries. She shot a bright, malevolent look at her son-in-law. And anyway Aubrey wasn't much of a catch. What a dour bat of a man! If he thinks so much of his sculpture, then why doesn't it sell? If he felt for the people, the people would feel for him. If he built bridges, she thought, I could understand him better. Pauline only admired him, she doesn't understand him – and he? I don't think he ever loved her, only the Idea of her, the Idea of being married. He used her discontent to lever off the top of her mind and pour in his own mad theories. Now he was trying to keep Dennis out of the war; away from his friends.

'Mother,' the voice was impatient, 'you're dreaming, dear. Won't you eat your apple-tart? Dennis, pass the cream to your grandmother.'

But her mother was rising. 'I must lie down,' she said, 'the sun . . . ' Slowly she went from the room, the invisible sparring was too much for her. When the door was closed, Aubrey said, aggressive in defeat:

'So you're going to be a hero, eh? I shan't cheer for you when you are dead or decorated.'

'Oh, God,' said Dennis. Sitting there, it seemed to him that his life was a series of different rooms; town, country, endless talk. Being ashamed to bring his school friends home, his parents were so 'queer'. 'Oh, God,' he said again. 'I want to be *normal*. I want to be everything you're not. I want to be a lawyer – settled . . .' He stopped.

His parents were watching him.

He rose.

'I don't want to disappoint you, mother,' he said, appalled at their immobility. 'I . . .' But he had to leave them, stumbling in haste to the door.

Pauline and Aubrey were staring at each other, alone in an empty room.

* * *

Dennis found his grandmother on the shady terrace. All the doors of her mind were opening and shutting. She could control them no longer.

> *You've ruined my life, mother.*
> *You've imposed your will on me, on us all.*
> *You don't understand . . .*
> *I'm leaving home, going to live with . . .*

Now it was Dennis. 'What's wrong with us all, Gran?' he was saying. 'I can't do what they want. I can't. It will break mother's heart, but . . .'

'Hearts never break, my boy,' said his grandmother, closing the doors one by one. 'Never.'

But he was not listening.

'I want security, Gran,' he was saying. 'I hate to see the tripe father has to turn out. He'll not be an artist at all very soon.'

'Yes, you're like me.' An old woman at the end of her life, seeing all things, at last the pattern fitted. With ancient malice she saw two unreal figures go down the lawn towards the orchard. We, the people, endure, she thought.

And the boy beside her bent his head as if he would weep at the ordinariness of himself, and of the world that needed him.

FIRSTBORN

□□□□□□□

Shifting her baby on to the other arm, Ruby looked about her. Everything the same. Not one tree flowering differently from the time she and Jim had made the walk over the common, round the pond and back by the tennis courts, their evening ritual.

The sun, scattered by April gustiness, had blown the gorse bushes into sudden blossom, and the nutty scent of them plunged her back into schooldays. Walking along that very path she had swung her hat by the elastic and quoted Shelley, almost suffocated by the enchantment of her rendering. The trees she had climbed seemed shrunken now, and maybe the blackberry bushes had never really concealed mazes of dark prickliness.

'Ruby!'

The voice was very much of the present. It came, astounded to her ears.

'Why, Ruby . . . you don't mean to say . . . ?'

The little lean woman's bright eyes, beaded like a woodpecker, peered at the babe. 'I didn't even know you were married!'

33

Only Mrs. Beavis's voice could produce such inflections of curiosity, disbelief and delicious shock. Suppose Ruby were *not* married! What a retailing: what nods, becks and stares the news would cause when she told the Bridge Club on Wednesday. She could imagine herself leaning forward over the table. 'Who *do* you think I saw?' She might even glance at a hand or two and make sure of winning the rubber . . . She'd like that butter dish Mrs. Patrick was offering as first prize.

But Ruby's voice, calm and a little amused, dissipated the vision.

'Oh, yes. Quite a while now. Jim had to go into the Army.'

Mrs. Beavis nodded, her mind busy. Jim? There were several possibles in the neighbourhood.

'Ah yes,' she sighed. 'Aren't things dreadful? My Beryl's in the A.T.S. now. Has a lot of fun. And how old is your little girl, or is it a boy?'

She fell into step with Ruby, chattering, and hoping to wake the baby up by clucking loudly.

'I suppose you're on your way to see your mother?'

Ruby laughed to herself as she left her at the corner of London Road. Wouldn't you like to know, she thought. Poor mother. She had resented the marriage too much to spread it abroad.

Ruby wondered how she would be received. After seeing her mother, she had promised Jim to take the baby along to his people. Neither of the two families liked each other in the least, each feeling that their child could have done better if they had waited longer. The two mothers had only met once, and Ruby well remembered the occasion. They had come to grips over the cradle. Mrs. Cradock had said the baby had her son's remarkably intelligent head and fine ears, and Mrs. Bowles responded by pointing out the firmly moulded mouth and chin. 'Ruby gets that from her father,' she said grimly. They had not arranged a second meeting.

Pushing open the green gate of her mother's house, she unconsciously braced herself.

'How tired you look, Ruby!' was her mother's first remark on opening the door. 'You've brought that dear baby – how *did* you get here?'

In the dining-room Ruby sat down with relief and laid the sleeping child on her lap. She threw her hat and gloves on the table.

'Oh, by train, then I walked.'

'You walked across the common! Doris, do you hear that? Ruby walked across the common! Why didn't you take a taxi?'

'Don't be absurd, Ada.' A thin woman, with an air of false youth about her, came into the room. 'There's no taxi-rank. You should have taken a bus to the end of the road, and I'd have met you. I'd have liked to carry the dear little tiddlums.' Her cragged pale face grew grotesque as she swooped towards the baby. 'And how is he? How is he?' Her voice rose thinly and woke him up. Seeing a stranger thrust directly above him, he broke into a howl. Immediately Aunt Doris whisked him up.

'What is it, my boofuls? Has Mummy left a pin to prick him?' Another idea struck her, and she eyed Ruby with suspicion. 'Or is he hungry?' She broke off to pat him on the back. 'Yes, he wants his din-din, don't you, Auntie's old pet?'

'He's not fed till two, Auntie,' Ruby said. 'He must sleep until then.' She held out her arms for the child, surprised at her own firmness. Surely they would concede her the right to manage her own baby. But no, Aunt Doris had definite ideas.

'Poor little chap,' she protested, giving him a smacking kiss. 'He can't lay all that time. Do you remember Mrs. Gunter's children, Ada? Their heads went flat with too much lying down.'

Ruby's years of home life forbade her to make the sharp remark that came to mind. Instead she glanced appealingly at her mother, who as usual looked dazed with her sister's unceasing flow of talk.

'I'll rock him,' said Aunt Doris. 'You leave him to me.'

'It *is* Ruby's baby,' said Mrs. Bowles. 'She has her own way of bringing him up . . .'

'Ruby's no more than a baby herself!' flashed back her sister. 'You can't tell me anything about children. Didn't I look after all Mama's while you and Florrie were out at business? And didn't I look after your two when you and Fred went away?'

The baby's cries drowned her voice and she laid him on a chair, examined his napkin, exclaimed in horror and demanded a dry one.

'*I'll* pin it, Ruby,' she said stiffly. 'What a strange way to fold a napkin. He'll go bandy. But I won't interfere. Your way's your way, I suppose. You always were self-willed.'

Ruby felt herself stripped of maturity. There she was back in a pinafore, being told to listen and not answer back pertly. Staring at Aunt Doris's back she thought: they'd like to do the same to my son when the gooing and pretty-sweet-baby period is over . . . Then, as in her childhood, she gave up and went with her mother into the kitchen, hating the proprietary air with which her aunt pinned the napkin.

'How's Jim?' asked Mrs. Bowles, peering mistily into a saucepan of boiling potatoes.

'Oh, he's on leave now,' said Ruby, who was looking into the garden. 'He's fine.'

'Then why didn't he come with you?' The question came swiftly; the same tone she had used when in the old days she had wanted to catch her daughter out in a lie. Ruby replied out of the deep knowledge of the past – habit forming soothing words.

'He had to see about his uniform. He's an officer now, you know.' She looked once more into the garden, moving the jam-jar with the mop in it to lean farther out of the window.

'Where's the buddleia tree, mother?'

'Dad dug it up,' replied Mrs. Bowles, grim in uneasy self-defence. 'It blocked the light from his greenhouse.'

For years Ruby had pleaded for the tree. It had transformed the rather barren garden with its puffs of pollen breezed from the swinging flowers. But Dad had waited until there could be no unpleasantness about it, and then had quietly done what he always intended doing . . .

'How is Dad?' Ruby inquired, without interest.

'Worried as usual about his business,' her mother replied, as if resenting that her husband could be in any other state. 'Now you shouldn't be standing about. You put your feet up while I bring in the dinner. You need all the rest you can get with a baby to feed – otherwise you'll upset his digestion.'

During the meal, Ruby felt a vicious desire to eat nothing, although she knew the food had been carefully selected for her – indeed because of that. They were only thinking of the child – the better the food Ruby ate, the better the milk for the baby. She fended off her aunt's questions skilfully and insisted on going into the next room to feed her baby while the other two women washed up. She left as soon after as she could, feeling the atmosphere of domineering kindliness unendurable.

'Bring him again, Ruby!' her mother called from the doorstep. 'Take a taxi next time!'

'Take care of yourself – and if you're in a muddle any time, give me a ring!' Aunt Doris's teeth flashed frantically in the sun as she shouted fresh adjurations after her.

Ruby walked up the street feeling as hot and embarrassed as if she were once more off to a Sunday School treat, bearing her large package of sandwiches. She rang at her mother-in-law's door and hoped with all her heart she would be out. She was thoroughly tired by the silent battle with her mother and aunt. How did I live at home so long? she thought, as she heard Mrs. Cradock's footsteps trotting up to the door.

'Why, Ruby my dear, how nice to see you! And how well you and the baby look!'

For a moment Ruby was warmed by the welcome. Here at least was no grudging incredulity as to her right to be a mother. She smiled and went before Mrs. Cradock into the garden, imagining the plump dipping and shooing that was going on behind her. When she was seated, Mrs. Cradock insisted on bringing her a cup of tea. 'I've made one for

Mrs. Harris next-door,' she smiled, and disappeared behind the trellis that hid the scullery. On emerging again she approached the fence that separated the two gardens and called with careful sing-song:

'Mrs. Har-ris! Mrs. Har-ris!'

Almost immediately a grey head appeared over the wall. It was Mrs. Harris. Her face fell with surprise at the sight of Ruby and the child.

'Dear me, you're not up already?' she said. 'Thank you, Mrs. Cradock. I was fifteen weeks on my back.' Her thin face settled into depressed lines. 'You never know what's going to happen in the future if you don't take care after the baby's born.' She looked curiously at Ruby. 'You *are* all right?' she said at last, grudgingly, as if finding it impossible to believe that Ruby's straight and strong young body could bear such slight witness to what, for her, had been a lifetime plaint.

'Of course she's all right,' said Jim's mother. 'She had the best of care, and Jim doesn't let her do too much . . . how is Jim, my dear?'

Mrs. Cradock could never bear any vague slight to be cast on her son, so it was unthinkable for his wife to be the object of sympathy. Now she approached the baby, who was wide awake and grinning windily.

'We're so glad he's an officer now,' she said. 'It makes such a difference – breeding always tells, doesn't it?' She picked the child up and bore him off to the fence. 'Isn't he the image of Jim?' she demanded. 'A real Cradock. You should be proud, Ruby.'

Fury made Ruby clatter her cup and saucer to the grass. A little hysterically she saw herself producing more and more Cradocks, bigger and better Cradocks, all the years of her life, and becoming prouder and prouder as they all manifested unmistakable Cradock tendencies . . . just then her father-in-law came into the garden. He had retired from his stockbroker's business and filled his time by taking schoolgirls across the common to buy them sweets, listening with pleasure to their anecdotes. His other amusement was cracking jokes with young married women. Altogether Ruby disliked him. Now he came across to her and kissed her cheek. He had always liked her soft skin.

'Well, well, my dear. How're things?' He gave the remark mysterious portent by a nicely timed wink. 'Not going to give us another grandson just yet, eh?' He slid a wicked glance to his wife. 'One at a time, eh, Mother?'

Mrs. Cradock turned from the fence. Her face was flushed with the exertion of entertaining the baby and she was pleasantly shocked by her husband's question.

'Go on with you, Tom,' she said, with a half-glance at Mrs. Harris. 'Isn't he awful?' she appealed, proudly sharing her husband's awfulness with the other two women.

Just then the sun and too much admiration made the baby vomit, and with a flutter of alarm Mrs. Cradock deposited him in Ruby's lap.

'Oh dear, oh dear,' she said anxiously, 'I do hope he's not going to have a weak stomach like Jim . . . How is his digestion, Ruby? Do you still feed him yourself?'

'Yes,' said Ruby, and this time she was really angry. 'I think he's been over-stimulated.' She addressed her son defiantly, personally, and it gave her immense joy to feel how far away in reality these other people were. 'Come on, sonny-jiminy,' she said. 'It's time we went home.'

She gathered up her things, and rose to go, refusing Mr. Cradock's offer of escort to the train.

It was late afternoon now and she breathed with relief as she once more trod among the pungent brassy gorse on her way to the station. What an awful, awful day it had been! And she had started out so gaily, eager to show her son off to everyone – but they, instead of applauding at a distance, had crowded in upon her, treading inside the charmed circle that was her life with Jim; had crushed, snatched and defiled with their commonplaces.

Sitting in the train, she intercepted glances from fellow-passengers, but refused to meet their eyes and listen once more to talk about the dear little baby. She saw her reflection in the window as they passed through a tunnel, and like a dark hand clutching her stomach, the thought came to her: am I then just 'woman and child'? One of the millions of drab creatures living for their children alone, with no will to live apart? Do I exist, not as Ruby, the centre that is me, but as just another wife bearing her man children, feeding him and keeping a home clean? The events of the afternoon answered yes, you are. She saw the beaded curiosity in Mrs. Beavis's eyes. The thrusting yet forever thwarted kindness of her aunt; the faded, embittered apathy of her mother; the yielding femality of Mrs. Cradock – surely she did not belong to this tight female world? A world of unconscious and eternal submission to the male – the ludicrous delight in procreation, their own and other people's, to make another human being in the likeness of man, which is the likeness of God, and another, and another . . .

Ruby looked down at her son, suddenly hating him. He and Jim between them had made her into just another woman. Meals for Jim and washing for the baby – it was all part of the grinding down process . . .

She walked past the door of her house more than once, although her arms were aching with the weight of the baby. She was trying desperately to bring herself to face Jim – but how could she, engulfed as she was in hatred for him and his child?

She was slowly approaching once more when the front door opened and Jim appeared. He came half-running, then stopped at the look on her face. 'Ruby,' he said, staring at her hard. 'Ruby, you're dead beat – the tea's made.'

Ruby was dazed. She found herself led up the path, into the house. Suddenly she realised Jim had taken the baby from her arms and had laid him somewhere, perhaps anywhere.

'The baby, Jim,' she said.

Her husband turned. He looked vague in his concern. But it was not concern for the baby. She knew that positively when she saw his eyes, loving her.

'We'll have some tea together,' he said. 'The baby can wait.'

WOMAN ABOUT THE HOUSE

◻◻◻◻◻◻◻

All night long the heavy lorries raced up the road towards the North. The road ran almost the length of England, straight as an architect's dream, passing from murky southern towns, over pastureland, flat fen country, purple heather stretches; mounting bridges, skirting mountains, until it reached the towns again, the grey stone Scottish cities.

James Munday lay in the brass-knobbed bed beside his wife and sighed as the room gave its customary tremor and the curtain swung heavily against the windowpane. His thoughts followed the drumming of tough tyres on to the next town, then, because the country beyond was strange to him, his mind slid back to this room, this bed – to this woman who was his wife, and whose breathing even in sleep was mean and tearful, as if she feared her breath would never return to her body if she gave too much out.

The village was one of the many lost among the flat spreading fields of cabbages and occasional scarecrows. The cottages stood like buffeted heaps of stone and rubble and the church in the midst of them was just a larger heap, strengthened with flint, still intact upon its Roman foundations, and bearing an elaborate gilt weathercock, given by a wealthy landowner in memory of his son.

A headlight travelled slowly over the ceiling, then was gone, leaving the room in deeper darkness. 'I'll get a job tomorrow,' James thought to himself, 'I'll show 'em.' But there was no force behind his inward protestation, his mind followed plans of revenge as often and as casually as his eyes roved after a perplexed bluebottle on the windowpane; as effortlessly as his ears picked up the thrum of night-tyres on the singing road. The lorries came from places beyond his knowing and passed on to others, equally unknown. James's room was to him as a lonely headland from which a watcher could note ships sailing beyond the horizon; their passing was an event, as the nine o'clock news was an event. They went into the night-wind with a dying crescendo of sound, and were lost.

His wife slept quietly beside him, her cheek swollen slightly. In the morning she would say: 'This owld neuralgia kept me awake all night. It's the wind round the back-door.' And James would know the guilt she wanted him to feel – after ten years of married life they still lived in the tiny damp labourer's cottage, two hundred years old and costing only two shillings a week. Her sister and mother had moved into the new council houses, each of which had a bathroom and kitchen and did not as yet let in damp. They felt that if James had been a Huntingdonshire man he would have done something about it: instead, he had come over the border from Northampton and had not kept a job for more than two years at a time ever since. He was a handsome man, his black springing hair and deep eyes giving him an alien look, which was emphasised by high cheek-bones and a well-blocked mouth. Lindy Briggs had married him on account of it. Out of disappointment she had conceived no children, thus giving the lie to his promise of virility. At thirty-seven he had the air of one ground into impotence; he spoke with difficulty, anticipating his wife's quick cut-in; he moved seldom, for his wife always got there before him. All that was left to him was to be alone in the night, alone in the darkness and the sounds born of it; a foreshortened squawk, a bellow; sometimes the hunting cry of an owl. But always the road, spreading across the land, taut as a violin string, waiting to be plucked into song.

The next morning James set off on his bicycle earlier than was necessary. He was heading for the nearest town where there was a job going laying cables. As he rode along slow thoughts formed themselves; thoughts he had been aware of for a month or so now, and which only came with the stilling of his wife's continual undertone of talk. He thought of the lorries. Behind each wheel was a man, a man who knew nothing of James Munday, the failure. If he should ever meet one of them, the man would know him just as a fellow to drink with, and judge him on that. He would not know that here was a man who had disappointed his wife, and who lived in a damp cottage, soon to be condemned; who even failed to raise any vegetables in the garden patch. Probably, and here James's throat contracted, probably he wouldn't care even if he did know. Riding slowly past the blossoming hedges he realised for the first time since the impulse had driven him out of the drabness of Northampton, that the world was a great place, there were many people in it. To be judged by a few was not to be condemned by them all. The cottage, the village, were only fractions of the world. There's a chance still, he thought.

He saw the manager of the works, and his new, almost jaunty confidence, got him the job. 'I like fellows to be keen,' said the manager.

For the first time in many years James went into the nearest public-house to celebrate. Business was not brisk, so the landlord talked whilst he polished glasses and shouted instructions to his daughter.

'Landed a job with the council, eh?' he said. 'Lucky fellow. They're good people to work for.' He went away to show his daughter how to pull the levers just so much and no more, otherwise the beer would flop and spill over.

James looked deep into the swirl of amber patterns in his glass. He ought to go back and tell Lindy. Slowly he drained it and put it down, but the landlord was on him before he could turn. 'Same again?' he asked. James nodded, and suddenly a phrase he had forgotten came into his mind. 'Have one on me,' he said. 'Why, don't mind if I do,' said the landlord. As he came back with the glasses, he leant forward and said, 'Want a room by any chance? there's one above empty; the missus cooks a good breakfast, can do you supper – '

After all, I've got the whole day, thought James; I'll do what I want. 'I'd like to see it,' he said.

As they mounted the stairs the landlord said, 'Was thinking it'd be easier for your job. Start early, don't you?'

'Eight-thirty,' James replied, 'I rode in this morning. Nine miles.'

'Nine miles! That's a tidy way night and morning.' The landlord opened a door off the landing. 'Here it is.'

The room was small, with oak furniture and a yellow carpet. The bed was by the window. In wonder, James found an electric-light switch and switched it on and off again.

'Pound a week, with breakfast and supper. Anyway, think it over.'

That night James returned to the small room over the bar. The village and Lindy, her sister and mother, had shrunk in importance: he had a job. He slept at once, and was awake early, ready for his breakfast. He felt a shock of warmth when he saw the landlord's wife bringing him egg and bacon, a smile on her face. It was years since his breakfast had been accompanied by any cheerfulness. At home the lamp would be alight, the day murky behind undrawn curtains, the cold wind round the back-door already plaguing Lindy.

He found his job took him about the countryside; he travelled in a van sometimes twenty miles away, repairing damaged cables and laying new ones. The number of small villages they passed amazed him. There were so many people living among the cabbage fields. In the evenings he drank and played darts with his workmates, proud to be with them, safe in their company.

It was a week before he remembered Lindy.

He lay late in bed on Sunday morning and thought about her. Not with anxiety, for the pity and indignation of her mother and sister would soothe that, she would be elevated in importance. She'll go and live with them, he thought with certainty. She's never really left them – always popping round the corner to ask them something. That was maybe why I failed so much. She's never been a real wife to me. It got me all muddled, having to be father and son to her.

That was it. She wanted it all ways. Many things were sorting themselves out in the quietness of his mind. Without the doleful sloth of the petted, scrawny cat, continually pregnant, the knowledge of kindling to be chopped, his hands had found a new cunning, and the foreman had complimented him on his neat work. The beer's doing me good, he thought to himself – I knew it was right for the digestion. At home he drank dark-brewed tea, which sometimes made his stomach clap and lurch into his bowels, or so it felt. Shall I send her a postcard? he thought. But as he considered the labour of it, he knew there was nothing to say. He had not written enough to know how to be glib in a few words.

Another week passed. He had to buy pyjamas and another pair of socks. He washed his shirt on Sunday. But something was troubling him. He was beginning to miss his own things about him, but there was another thing too. One evening in the bar he asked Tom, the landlord, whether the night lorries passed through the town.

Tom laughed. 'No, thank heaven,' he said, 'they bypass us, the noisy brutes. Streets too narrow for 'em. They want that great big road to skid about on.'

'Oh,' said James, and was silent.

After that he lay awake at night, trying to hear beyond the creaking quiet of the town, and reach the great road beyond. He imagined the tremor of the room, the play of light on the ceiling. The continued darkness depressed him. He began to worry about the lorries – suppose they had stopped running altogether?

After he had collected his wage packet at the end of the following week, he paid the landlord and got on his bicycle to ride the nine miles home. It was a wet night and the hedges gleamed as his lamp picked out the interlaced twigs. The sky was high, and clouds like cotton thread streamed across the moon. He cycled down the muddy lane and saw there was no light in the cottage. Although he had not expected there to be, he was relieved. Going round to the back door he found the key in the usual place under a pile of kindling, roughly chopped by Lindy. Stumbling, he went inside. The fire was out, but ready laid, the room empty, strange with its deadness and the absence of the cat. Drawing the curtains, James lit the lamp, then turned at once to the fire. He wanted to see the room as it usually was before he looked round.

He took more pleasure in lighting the fire than he had for a long while. It's good to do things for yourself, he thought, as he carefully arranged coal on the wood, and struck a match to it. The oven by the side of the grate was newly blacked, and he felt tempted to open it to see if the usual baked rice pudding was there. It was empty. He stared at the oven for a long while. This was the most final thing of all; Lindy had left him for good. With a feeling of shock and pain he stared round the room, automatically adjusting the wick of the lamp. The upright piano, his chair with the faded cushion, the brown curtain over the door leading into the parlour, chill with disuse. These things he saw in a good, a tender light. They were his. He had saved for them. These things alone had withstood the shipwreck of the years. It was good to be among them, they made him feel safe, as did the men with whom he passed his evenings.

On the piano was a white envelope. He opened it, and took out his wife's note.

'I've gone and you needn't think as I shall come back. How you will cook and do for yourself I don't know but it will serve you right. You needn't worry about me, not as if you would. I would rather help keep Mother alive than look after a good-for-nothing – Lindy.'

James read it through twice and sat down in the chair by the brightening fire. He put the kettle on the edge just over the flames, and for once no hand shot out to correct him. He looked at the note again and smiled, then suddenly roared with laughter, slapping his knees. 'Keep mother alive,' he said aloud, he picked up the Radio Times and turned the knob of the wireless. A jangle of ill-assorted instruments filled the room, another turn, and a heartbroken crooner cut across faint garbled foreign voices. The din startled him, and he wondered at the time when he had loved the noise and power of the small square box. Turning the knob lower, and choosing the news, he knew that now the full alien music had no place in his life – there was no voice to drown.

He prepared some tea for himself, taking infinite pleasure in the warming of the pot, the measurement of spoonfuls. Suppose I'll miss a woman about the house, he thought as he drank. Take some getting used to. He lit his pipe and lay back in the chair. Might get a dog. The idea pleased him, and he imagined serene evenings, the dog's head a warm patch on his knee. Old Banks next door'll look after him in the day

– that is, if he'll still speak to me. Wonder what Lindy's told folks? But he was not really concerned with what the village would think of him. There were many other villages, and many more people.

As he shaved that night it seemed to him the room was friendly, and his eyes brighter than for many years. He felt the energy of his youth stirring in his blood, and as he went upstairs to bed he was busy with plans. I'll see what can be done with the vegetable patch, he thought. Soil's good, there must be something – He stopped on the threshold of the bedroom, his candle flaring. The emptiness and whiteness of the room held no ghosts, it was as if he and Lindy, young and fresh, had never lain there together. Standing by the door he thought, with an odd slow sorrow: she never really gave herself to me, never. Mean about that, and mean about having children. Might hurt her – too delicate. The candle made deep shadows by the water-jug, and he closed the door, undressed and got into bed. I must wake up early tomorrow, he thought. There's a lot ahead of me.

Much later he was asleep, smiling at the ceiling which passing headlights patterned strangely. From the night outside came the sound of wet tyres churning along the sticky road.

TELL IT TO A STRANGER

□□□□□□□

The war had been on nearly three years when Mrs. Hatfield, on one of her periodic visits home, found a young reserve policeman whistling on her front doorstep and leaning against the splintered door. He had news for her: the house had been ransacked. After a moment's coldness in her stomach, Mrs. Hatfield raised her eyebrows.

'Perhaps you would allow me to come in and see for myself,' she said.

The young policeman knocked the door open and stood aside for her. He wondered how long she would take to dissolve into an understandable hysteria. But she went through the whole house, noting silver ornaments missing, seeing the drawers pulled out, photograph albums and old accounts lying with West Indian shells over the floor. Upstairs her linen savagely mauled, cashmere shawls gone, the one good fur cape. Cut glass bottles, beautiful wine glasses that responded finely to a flick of the thumbnail – this seemed the full extent of the haul. In her bedroom she stood in silence a long while. She saw that although her carpet was ripped across one corner it could be repaired. This was not a total loss – but by the evening it would be, when she told the story to her fellow-guests at Belvedere.

The policeman was saying: 'Helped himself to the whisky all right. Sergeant finished off the rest, he grinned amicably. 'Must've worked in a raid,' he said, and again grinned, this time in admiration. 'Some nerve.'

Really, thought Mrs. Hatfield through her preoccupation, if he wasn't a policeman I do believe he would become a criminal. She said curtly: 'I suppose you would like a list of the things missing?'

'Well, you don't have to do it at once, ma'am.' He was a little put out by her lack of emotion. 'But I'll have to ask you to step round to the station with me to have your fingerprints taken . . .' That touched her, pricked the present into her calm, and he felt obscurely pleased. It always got them that way. A look of horror, of flinching, came into her eyes. Again, the thought of the evening comforted her – how would they take it, she wondered.

'That's quite all right,' she said, and without another look at the furniture, now stripped of its shrouds, she went out into the streets with him.

That evening on the train she felt even more exhilarated than when she had seen the dogfight in the sky. How they had listened as she described the tiny metal flashes high over the town, how they had sighed when the smoke poured out, like lifeblood into the clear sky.

Mrs. Hatfield had moved out to Belvedere just before the bombing started, when it was a not very successful guest house, despite the palms in the coffee room and the planned garden. But when the guests at the promenade hotels saw the sun pick out the bitter spikes of barbed wire set in concertina rolls along the beach, and heard the cry of rising gulls as shells whistled deadly out at sea, every room at Belvedere was taken, and an annexe planned.

Sitting back in the blue-lighted train, Mrs Hatfield thought back over those two years. There was no doubt about it, she was a happier woman, more alive than she had ever been. It's a dreadful thing to say, she told herself, but this war's been a blessing to some. Hastily she brushed away all thought of the shadier blessings, and fixed firmly on the unemployed. You're happy when you're working, she thought. As the train stopped, the jerk shattered her conclusion: Jack had hated working. Although in the colonies you never did much anyway. I never could please him, she thought with sudden pain. She pleased the others, her friends now. Mr McAdam, Miss Blackett, Doreen, and Mrs. Kent. She almost loved Mrs. Kent, for indirectly all her happiness hinged on her. For if she had not kept on with Belvedere – Mrs. Hatfield almost shuddered.

'I've been ransacked, my dears, everything – ' slowly the train slid on its way, like a cowed animal, unobtrusive as possible. Then from the outer darkness the rise and fall of a distant siren swept across the country, starting from the coast, and as in a relay race, handing on the warning to towns nearer the capital.

For a moment Mrs. Hatfield felt panic, the country lay so dark either side of the track and there was no stopping. The clank and swing of wheels over points drowsed her into a numb sense of security. This could go on forever, this invisible rushing through dark fields, wooden stations, hidden towns

– it was all so effortless and smooth. She lifted her feet and looked at them; they were not walking, yet she was being carried incredible distances.

Almost imperceptibly another sound wove itself into the darkness, a gentle hum-humming, fast gaining on them. The train attempted to go even faster, but at this the humming increased until the whole countryside lay petrified under the heavy *throb-throb-throb*. Deliberately, delicately, the air rushed down, and somewhere to the right earth fountained up like oil from a gusher. Again, nearer the track this time, and clods of rich meadow grass and clay fell heavily onto the roof of the train, plastering windows and doors. A third and fourth followed swiftly, the full effect dulled by the soggy earth. Then came machine-gun fire, sharp and tearing as sudden rain on corrugated iron.

'This is war,' thought Mrs. Hatfield, and her heart lifted and throbbed in time with the great steel heart in the sky. But her feet were cold and numb and hung heavily on to the floor. She heard the guard go by, calling in a low voice, as if fearful of being overheard, 'All blinds down. Screen all lights. Jerry overhead.' He repeated this with flat authority as he ducked along the corridor. How stupid, thought Mrs. Hatfield; she almost laughed, a dry bad-tasting tremor of her tongue. Who else could it be? Doggedly the train went on. Passengers, white-lipped, told each other it was impossible to hit a moving object in the dark. Besides, the Hun flashboards weren't fitted with proper sights, everyone knew that.

In her compartment Mrs. Hatfield sat erect. For a moment she felt almost petulant; this was too much to tell. She could not allow this episode to crowd out the other. I have been ransacked, she told herself firmly. My beautiful wine-glasses, Jack's last present to me. But she was listening to the sudden quietness, the suspense throughout the whole train, spreading from carriage to carriage. The hum-humming was growing less. It was lost in the nightwind.

Immediately the corridors were filled with strung voices, some jaunty with relief, others low and shaken. The train had stopped. 'Good heavens,' said Mrs. Hatfield aloud. 'This must be my station.' She called from the doorway to make quite sure, and then got out of the train. It drew away silently, some of its windows broken by bullets which were now souvenirs. She watched it go, her ears still blocked with the noise of the thrumming sky.

Shaking a little, she went over the humped bridge and along the road. Overhead the wires sang between her and the faint moon, cold as the rime on the hedges.

'I'll be better when I get home,' she thought, and it warmed her to speak of Mrs. Kent, of Belvedere, as home. They were waiting for her, she knew it, waiting for her to walk in between the palms and bring them news of the world at war. News without the slickness and positivity of the radio, the newspapers, which contained, as they felt, an oblique reproach.

She had something to tell this time. Here was some real news, directly touching her, and through her, every person at Belvedere. The war had at last affected them personally; they were no longer grouped outside it, they shared in the general lawlessness. Lack of respect for property. What are we coming to? Police finishing off the whisky, wouldn't be surprised if – and so it would grow, filling more than an evening, filling the days, recreating their lives, and more important, affirming their belief in the past.

As Mrs. Hatfield hurried down the lanes she felt exultant, almost like an envoy back from untold perils. She looked ahead and thought: I must have come the wrong way. For there was a glow in the sky. A haystack, she thought again. Then she stopped thinking and hurried on, for somehow she knew it was not a haystack burning, and she never came the wrong way.

She ran into the drive of Belvedere, and said stupidly, 'But there's nothing there.' It was the wooden annexe burning, the flames driving back the ambulance men and village firemen.

'You can't go any nearer, ma'am,' said one of them, struggling with a hose.

'Where are they?' asked Mrs. Hatfield. She was white and the bones showed through the flesh of her cheeks. The man shook his head and motioned to the heaps of bricks and blazing rafters. 'Better ask the ambulance people,' he said, and wrenched the hose round.

'They can't drop bombs on Belvedere,' cried Mrs. Hatfield, with tears suddenly released and streaming down her face. She started to shout, to drown the flames with noise, 'Doreen! Mrs. Kent! I've got some news – some news – ' One of the ambulance men came over from a group of silent people.

'Now then, now then,' he said, 'we're doing our best. Got one or two out, but they can't do much until the fire dies down.'

Mrs. Hatfield ran to the stretchers she saw on the ground. A maid, one of the newer arrivals, a porter. 'Chance in a million,' she heard one of the onlookers say.

'I've been ransacked,' said Mrs. Hatfield to herself, gently, conversationally, 'ransacked.' She looked round at the people staring at the fire. They would not care. She ran up to a pile of rubble – maybe it was the lounge – and started to tear away the bricks and glass. As the hole grew deeper a childhood tale flashed through her mind. *The Emperor has ass's ears*, the poor little barber who had to shout his secret into the earth, and the song of the corn repeating it. *The Emperor has ass's ears*.

The firemen watched her incredulously.

'There's pluck for you,' said one. 'Poor old girl, friend of hers, I suppose.'

He went over to her. It was singeing hot even here. He seized her beneath the armpits.

'You can't!' he shouted as the flames found fresh ground.

Mrs. Hatfield looked up at him.

'My lovely wine glasses,' she said.

LULLABY

She had never been quite sure about it, but he was convinced.

'It's a great idea, a marvellous idea,' he said, 'but of course if you don't want to come out with me when I'm on leave, just say so.'

So she had given in. She always did. Life with him was precarious; always had been. She had sudden terrible fears of him leaving her. Suddenly walking from the room, out of the house, knowing he had gone on to some other life and needed no one. 'It's being in the air so much, doing so much flying,' she thought. 'It must do something to you.' Hanging on to a cloud and never coming down – only of course you fell through a cloud.

When they had the child it was better, for a time. Then the juggling began. She could keep them both spinning equably, dexterously, for a time; father and son, son and father, but then her hand would become tired, the trick fail. This was such a time, so she said yes, and they went to a friend of his who had cashed in on the pre-war vanity of people who wanted their voices recorded.

'Only a few left,' he said. Wistfully he looked over the wax discs. 'Still, it was fun while it lasted. Did I tell you the story of the man who was too nervous to propose on the spot – ?'

'Yes,' he was told.

'Oh.' He was obviously disappointed. 'Well, what are you going to do?'

It was explained.

'Why, that's wonderful!' he exclaimed. 'That's – come on, let's hear you.'

They tried it out that evening and sat listening in the next room. The child was in his cot, but was talking to himself in a queer half-language of his own. He sang a little, chuckled and made astonished noises. Then the record was started.

'Go to sleep, darling,' came his mother's voice from the black box. There was a pause, then 'Hush now, bye-byes.' The baby stopped murmuring and settled down. Then the voice said: 'Everything's all right, Mama's here.' The child seemed to be asleep, but they let the record run to the end. 'It won't disturb him,' she whispered, and gazed as the voice sang, a little self-consciously spinning from under the needle. 'What's to be done with the baby son – '

A little breathlessly the record stopped, clicked. The next room was silent.

'There!' he said triumphant. 'That's all right, isn't it? He only needs to hear your voice and off he goes.' She smiled. It did seem a good idea.

'Come on,' he said, 'let's go.'

They did it once or twice after that, until he had to return to his station. But he couldn't forget it. 'You must make one for me,' he wrote. But somehow she never did. She hated her voice spinning off the black disc; she felt as if her whole being was caught beneath the sharp needle, dragged round like a piece of fluff in the shining grooves.

When he next came on leave he said: 'Sanders tells me we positively must see that film at the Empire. It's tremendous.'

'The Empire?' she said. 'It's a long way.'

He looked at her with the peculiarly blank expression he assumed when he was determined to do something in the face of any obstacle.

'We've got the record,' he said. 'We'll be home by ten if we go early.'

So that evening she put the baby to bed earlier, and they set the record off as they went out of the door. In the hall, he stopped suddenly and caught her in his arms. 'You're sure you feel all right about leaving him, darling?' he asked. 'I'm a selfish brute.'

She laughed. Her fear was always there, but it must not spoil his evening, and the idea of him being worried somehow strengthened her.

'He'll be all right,' she said firmly. 'Don't worry.'

Together they walked down the road.

'What a wind!' she said.

Back in the nursery the wind in a sudden gust shifted aside the blackout curtain they had always meant to fix. The house stood on a corner and took the full force of any storm.

'More of a gale,' he said.

The nightlight, usually unwavering in its saucer, flickered unsteadily; a tiny edge of the curtain was blown across and remained a little above it. From his cot the baby watched the flame grow bright. He chuckled and sang to himself. Then his mother's voice came gently. 'Go to sleep, darling.' He turned over and put his thumb in his mouth. But the brightness still fascinated him; he wanted to tell his mother about it. 'Hush now, bye-byes.' Obediently he closed his eyes. A sudden intensity of light swept across his eyelids; the curtains were blazing. He opened his mouth to scream with sudden inexplicable fear, but across the lighted room came the trusted voice that was with him all day, 'You're quite all right. Mama's here.' He looked about, where was she?

He didn't like it. The wind rushed round the corner and swept the fire across to the chest of drawers – cottonwool, picture-books. The baby was standing in his cot now, gripping the rail and shaking, his eyes wide and black with fear, almost islanded by flame and across the room came the lullaby ' . . . we'll put him away for a rainy day . . .'

As they got off the bus, she gripped his arm. The journey had passed in silence, but now it was as if she lay beneath the sharp needle, caught in the spinning grooves.

'Did you hum that song we made up for the baby just then?' Her voice was edged, and he looked at her, startled.

'No,' he said, 'I could have sworn you were singing it.'

For a moment they looked at one another. Then:

'Taxi!' he shouted. 'Taxi!'

SUBJECT FOR A SERMON

□□□□□□□

She leaned forward on her toes, white-gloved hands clasped. In her navy uniform, with hair cut close about her ears, she looked like an earnest schoolgirl.

'You know,' she was saying with controlled frankness, 'I shall enjoy the second part of this programme so much better, having spoken.' The hot faces in the little church hall relaxed into grins of sympathy. Not that she hadn't enjoyed the *first* half, Lady Hayley explained, but – an expressive gesture completed the sentence for her. She glanced disarmingly towards the sides of the platform. Reproachful faces stared at her from slits in the odd curtains that formed the wings, curtains now bulging with the jostling bodies of those who had already performed. *And* she was touched by the efforts they had all made, organisers, performers, everyone in the small village had contributed – done their bit. Her voice grew deeper and more fluent. *Her* thanks, she said, were nothing compared to what the men would say when they came home. It meant such a lot to them to know that *everyone* – men, women, yes, *and* children, was doing something to bring victory nearer.

Miss Pollett nodded, looking round at her Guides. She was standing with one foot on the platform steps to balance them. She nodded and looked at her girls. Then she motioned some little boys away from the platform edge. One of them had already sat on the curtain and now it hung in a perilous loop above where Lady Hayley would have to step down from the platform. And Miss Pollett felt possessive towards Lady Hayley, she was taking her home to spend the night. She glanced round the hall, it was crowded. With relief she noted the vicar at the back, he would keep order on the window-sills – how boys loved climbing up on to them. She tried to catch his eye, but he was looking intently at the speaker.

'. . . so I know you won't let me down, will you?' Her clasped hands were coming forward now, in a pretence of anxiety. The speech was coming to an end.

Judging her moment, Miss Pollett sprang up on to the platform so that Lady Hayley could not get past her to the steps. She held up a hand against the dying applause.

'I just want to say,' she began, hand now tucked familiarly into her belt, 'that we have a special reason for thanking Lady Hayley for being with us tonight.' She paused, and her distinguished visitor looked down at her black polished shoes, a shy gesture. 'It is this. Yesterday she learned that her son was coming home on embarkation leave. I told her she must not think of coming, but – Lady Hayley won't mind me quoting her words – she told me over the phone, "I've always said the Red Cross comes first, now's my chance to prove it." And as her train left the station, her son's train pulled in.' Miss Pollett stopped and involuntarily caught the Vicar's eye. He wore an

66

expression she knew well; he had found a subject for his sermon – she must have just given it to him. In his joy he was leading the renewed applause and there were murmurs of sympathy. Lady Hayley smiled and blushed, led the way off the platform and the concert went on.

As they drove home after dropping the last Brownie, Miss Pollett started to talk. It was as if the tiredness of her body, the excitement of having Lady Hayley to herself in the dark, rattling car released some suppressed verbal energy. But as her companion continued silent, her eyes closed and remnants of the vivacious smile wan on her mouth, Miss Pollett found herself talking faster than she had intended. Her voice became louder, she put overtones and undertones into it; sometimes she gestured with one hand on the wheel, laughed excitedly. She did not want to talk about the concert, but almost involuntarily she told how the whole thing was the Guides' own idea – she had nothing to do with it except sell a few tickets and of course, get Lady Hayley down to bless the occasion as County Organiser. The parents had trained the small Brownies, made all their dresses – no-coupon muslin, of course, weren't they wonderful? . . .

As she at last eased the car through the garage doors her voice ceased as automatically as the engine, and for a moment she savoured the healing silence, felt the echoes of talk dying in her head. Then she turned to her companion. Lady Hayley's face was quite blank, a little crumpled. After a pause the charming voice spoke out of the darkness and they went from the garage to the house, but Miss Pollett could not help feeling a silent judgement had been passed on her.

They drank the coffee that had been kept warm on the hearth, wrapped in blue flannel, and although Lady Hayley said, 'Wonderful, I think they are all simply wonderful,' Miss Pollett could no longer respond. She had nothing more to say. It was as if the party were over, everything flat. Also she had a strange feeling that if the other coffee cup had not been on the table, the cap beside it, she could have believed herself alone in the room. And to allay the disturbing feeling that she could never get past that quick smile – to prevent it pushing her away – she asked about the morning train. The 7.30 was the earliest, if she was not too tired . . .

'I must get that one,' replied Lady Hayley, 'I have a meeting at noon.' Then, as if some expression on the other's face made her remember something, she added quickly, 'John will understand.'

* * *

John Hayley sat outside the stables, cleaning an old gun of his father's. The mists were curling away from the other side of the valley and there was a promise of heat. Round three sides of the house the pines and firs were still wet from the night rain, their heavy foliage curiously unseasonable. As the sun grew hotter the scent of early wallflowers dispersed the tang of the trees, and the old sunk cobblestones of the yard dried patchily.

He called over his shoulder to someone inside: 'This double summertime certainly lets you in on the dawn, Griffiths.' He spoke in Welsh and without waiting for a reply, ducked his head, for he was a tall youth, and went through the low door into the gloom where an old man sat among harness and guns.

Almost caressingly Griffiths answered him. 'A pity there's no horse now for you on mornings like this.' He looked through the door of the harness room down into the long, cool stable and nodded to each empty stall. 'Glendwyr, Gwyneth, Mad Robert – ' he shook his head and rubbed at the saddle he was working on.

'Hand me another,' said John abruptly as he laid the gun he was carrying on the rough table by the window. The old man selected one for him and with a frown the lad said: 'This needs oil very badly,' and going outside he started to look it over with care. After a while he became aware of the sun on his face and smiling for the first time that morning, he rose, stretched, and with the gun still over his arm, strolled off to the front of the house.

Here everything was startlingly different. The ground sloped abruptly away in lawns to the winding road below. There were no trees and the wide glass windows drank in the sun. He glanced in at the front door, placed at the side corner to protect the hall from the direct heat that would beat down once the sun was fairly up over the far mountains. The oaken hall seemed always to be cool and dark. It was long as a corridor and the stuffed victims of his father's gun were quiet in their glass cases, and until a door was opened somewhere inside no gleams were struck from the unsheathed swords and sabres hanging high up near the ceiling.

After a moment's hesitation he set off down the main drive. The little train had just passed through the station, leaving its fragmentary signature against a blue sky. The rhododendrons were a sight, he thought, picking one idly as he went on to the main gates. A pity he had missed the daffodils, they must have flowered early. As he saw his mother coming up the slope from the station he felt irritated at missing the daffodils and cut at the withered brown trumpets and drooping leaves with his gun. Then she waved and he threw the gates open ceremoniously and ran to meet her.

'You look tired,' he said accusingly, after they had kissed and were walking up together, she on his arm, her fingers light on the rhododendron flower.

'Why did you not come to the station to meet me?' she asked, looking up at him almost girlishly.

'I might almost ask why you – ' but her hand was over his mouth, her eyes reproachful.

'John, dear.'

He laughed against his will. 'You always know what I'm going to say,' he said half-sulkily. 'All the same . . .'

'There's no ammunition in the house now,' said his mother, catching sight of the gun. 'Did you want to go off shooting?'

'Oh, later, perhaps,' he replied carelessly, 'actually I scrounged some before I came away, hope it'll fit.'

She said nothing to this, but disengaged her arm quickly as the telephone bell rang out through the open door. She took off her cap when just inside the hall and ran firm fingers through her hair. As she moved to take up the telephone John picked up the cap and idly swung it round on one finger. His mother was only a moment: she made brief replies. 'No, no difference at all. Of course I shall be there. Yes, yes. Goodbye.' Then she made small pencilled notes on a pad near her hand.

'You know, darling,' he said as she rang off, 'I hate you in this cap. It's absurd somehow.' He glanced at her in sudden appeal. 'Look, won't you change into one of your frocks, come for a walk, early lunch and . . .'

Lady Hayley took the cap from him playfully and then with one turn of her strongly-knit, almost dumpy body, was on the first stair. With a little laugh she called back: '*I'm* not on leave, if you are, silly billy!'

When she came down again it was to find him smoking moodily on the terrace. She took his arm confidentially.

'I'm going to rest here a little if you will bring out a chair. Sit by me, I want to see how changed you are.'

She had combed out her hair and relaxing with her feet up John could imagine her, summers ago, in one of her green linen frocks, enjoying the sound of a lawn-mower somewhere below, and the hot energetic ping of unseen tennis balls.

'Well?' he asked at last, almost rudely, as he found her watching him.

She laughed and held out her hand for a cigarette. When he had lighted it she glanced down at the neat gold wrist-watch, half-hidden beneath her navy cuff.

'We shall have to start in about an hour,' she said. 'So we've time for a nice talk.' She closed her eyes, but her son said nothing. 'That is, if you haven't forgotten how to ride a bicycle.' Her voice was light and teasing.

71

'Where to?' asked John, beginning to tap on the gun-barrel with long fingers. His mother tried to keep her eyes away: she hated any purposeless movement.

'There is a blood transfusion meeting,' she said evenly. In the strong sunlight her face looked tired, as if the skin was stretched by too many smiles, too many alert, interested nods. 'We have made ourselves responsible in this county for at least two hundred and fifty donors. I thought . . .'

'You want me to talk to them? Tell them how the fellows appreciate it, eh?'

His mother looked at him. 'I don't care for your tone, John,' she said dryly. No doubt the army had coarsened him. 'Sometimes I think you have inherited your father's most unlovable traits.' In spite of a distaste for his drumming fingers and sprawled legs, she touched his arm. 'John, I know you've been through a lot. I know you are on leave, going abroad soon. But don't you see that for people like us duty is never finished? We can never relax, it is our privilege to lead. You are a lieutenant – '

'Captain now,' he murmured.

'And you never said a word!'

'Wanted to tell you last night. I was quite pleased about it then. But this morning – it doesn't seem important any more.'

'Well!' his mother leaned back. 'It is just that sort of attitude that is wrong. Always you see things in the wrong perspective. There are many things *I* do not like doing – Miss Pollett frays my nerves. I dislike long journeys under-taken in uncomfortable circumstances, I am nervous when on a bicycle. But if *I* did not do these things, who would? It is expected of my position – our lives are not our own, John.'

Her son looked at her curiously, and the set of her shoulders, the impenetrable reason moulding her face, set up a wonder in him. This wonder had been stirring for months, a half-understood, uncomfortable thing. What would she do, what would the people like her do, if they once realised that their lives were indeed their own? Had she, had they, the courage to take them up and see?

Impulsively he said, 'That's just it, mother, that's just where I feel you're wrong. You wouldn't dream of letting the people round here organise their own schemes. And you don't really care about them; you don't want to *know* them, they're just a mass of faces in a church hall to be talked at, and exhorted. You're only interested in maintaining your own position, and seeing that they keep to theirs. They're fair game for pennies, but you wouldn't recognise one of them in the street afterwards.' He looked angrily at her. 'I've lived among them, mother. I know what they think about people like us. I know what they're like and what they want – and it's nothing we represent. We've had our chance as leaders of society, and lost it.'

His mother made a great noise with her feet as she lifted them down from the stool to make room for the tray of coffee a maid brought out. From habit he remained silent until the girl had disappeared again round the stone coping. 'You can't believe they're fed up with us, can you? Even if Gwen had poured the coffee down our necks? But I tell you that when the war ends, that's the end of our kind, too. They'll just sweep us away and choose their own leaders.'

He took up his gun again and began tapping it lightly on the ground between his legs. He was cold with a sudden fear; never before had he spoken to his mother like this. But she only looked amused.

'I suppose you still allow yourself the luxury of cream and sugar in coffee, my boy?' He went a dull red and threw the gun on the ground. How many times in his childhood had she spoken to him in exactly that controlled, bantering tone? Usually it effectively silenced the jerky spasms of talk that had marked the beginning of the queer, groping independence and sudden insight of his adolescence.

'I can do without it, if that's what you mean,' he said ineffectually. 'In the Naffy – '

'Oh, come. No boasting, John.' She handed him his cup with a slightly raised eyebrow, and he knew he was being invited to laugh with her at himself, at his boorishness. Laugh, maybe kiss her and give in. But he merely scuffled his feet and took the cup gracelessly. Lady Hayley watched him, her face settling into a frown.

'Don't worry, John,' she said, her voice hard. 'They'll never sweep *me* away. Why, you make me feel like a bad old Russian landowner wielding a knout! Do be sensible and realise that this fancy of yours to be – shall I say – one with the people, is just a phase; like Dora what's-her-name at Castle Mount wanting to be a nun. Young people are all the same, only when I was young all the girls wanted to be like Mrs. Eddy or Sylvia Pankhurst. And the boys ached to go to Paris, affect flopsy ties and a French mistress, then come back talking languishingly of *fin-du-siècle* . . .'

Perhaps it was the carelessness with which she pronounced the phrase that roused John. It seemed to sum up, even more than the use of the weary cliché, her tolerant, humorous dismissal of anything new, anything foreign. Out of shame for her careless mispronunciation he retorted that times were changed; that he was twenty, not sixteen like Dora what's-her-name, and that dilettantism had died a natural death after the Great War, that –

'Oh, how dreary, all this talk of the times!' exclaimed Lady Hayley. 'If you're serious – which I doubt, no young man is *ever* serious at twenty – then *go* to the people, become one of them. Eat their fish and chips, drink their cocoa. Wear a muffler and learn to lounge against a lamppost. But I warn you that if they don't accept *me* for what I am – a leader with generations of experience behind me – how much less will they accept you, trying to be something that does not exist. A canary let out among sparrows!' She put the tray decisively on the ground and replaced her legs with a sigh. 'No, my boy. We've got to make a stand. And you must take up your difference with courage, otherwise you'll find you're a misfit. And there's nothing so boring as that.' She looked at him oddly, then went on, 'I noticed a book on the French revolution in the dining room, you'd been reading it. Well, there's a good lesson for you. The aristocrats didn't really lose, because the mob could only cut off their heads. And ultimately that's such a small thing.' Glancing at her watch, she rose to her feet. 'I must go now, I can see you don't want to come with me.

But think about what I've been saying. You can't shirk the issue, John.'

Quickly she turned from him, left him sitting there.

* * *

That afternoon before she came home from the meeting John wandered round to the stables again. But they were empty, the harness room neat with the saddles back on their nails and smelling of the polish Griffiths had used. He was suddenly warmly grateful to the old man for this unnecessary task, then, looking round idly, he saw his fishing rods stacked in one corner. For the first time it struck him as strange that they should not be in what used to be his father's study – for after all, they were originally his father's rods, left to him. Then he remembered that this was now being used as a drying room for herbs collected and brought in by volunteers. All the same, it was somehow disquieting to find them outside the house altogether . . . perhaps they were only being over-hauled. It might be a good idea to do a bit of fishing. More than ever he felt the need to be voluntarily submerged in the silence and invulnerability that, as a fisherman, he could cast about himself.

Once settled in the woods, however, beside the river, the fine day turned to rain, and crouching up his shoulders, he shifted into shelter to watch the shimmer of the two waters meeting: rain and river, from now on indivisible. Once again he was feeling bitter towards his mother. Thinking: at least my collection of flies is intact. It's a wonder she hasn't presented them to the Prime Minister on his birthday. As the rain cleared he cast in his line, but the peace he hoped for was not to be found in this stream, in these woods. Perhaps not in this time at all. Funny, he had known this leave was going to be all wrong from the moment he had looked out of the train on to the empty platform – of course, old Jones the stationmaster was there. Good old Jones, with the silver plate in his head, nineteen-sixteen relic.

He sat watching the river, his mind clogged with rancour. Tidying him away, just like his father – that's what she was doing. His rod trembled and he drew it up; the hook and fly were gone. Carefully he wound up his line and started back through the woods. He wished he had a dog at his heels.

His mother was already at the table when he came in, and they spoke very little during the meal. He wanted to bring up the matter of the rods, but feared to be soothed by her reasonable explanations. Instead he watched her, wishing she would ask him eagerly, curiously, what the strange half-world of the army was like. He wanted her to make tentative enquiries as to the girls he had met. He wanted to hear the anxious 'I hope, John . . .' which would make him into a man of the world, not a boy on his school holiday. But she did not speak, and as John looked at her, across the planned expanse of table he pondered how strange it was that one never thought about one's parents as separate people until they were dead, or it was too late to have a relationship with them anyway. Did they always see their children as beings from a different, a nursery world?

Lady Hayley moved into her favourite low chair by the window, and picked out a pack of patience cards that were always in a box on a small table there. She had wanted to tell him about the meeting, but his closed face stopped her, reminded her of his absurd and irritating mood of the morning.

'What did you do this afternoon, John?' she asked, laying out the cards neatly. One, two, three, face down. Yes, tonight it would be Sevens. 'By the way, the dean is coming . . .' she paused, a tiny hesitation which conveyed her meaning exactly. John had strolled over to the windows, and was standing as he had done a hundred times before, to watch the slow evening procession of clouds above the valley. Ponderous, impersonal, they passed in the form of ghost-porpoises, rolling snails, wisps of fish and formless old testament heads with their drifting, drowning beards. When he spoke, it was in the dean's social voice, which sounded as if he were discreetly gargling with the best port. 'Home is the hero, eh? Dear lady, you must be proud – '

He broke off abruptly as his mother swept the cards up. It was impossible to concentrate in such an atmosphere.

'John, I've never heard you speak this way before. Is it the men you've been mixing with?' Her voice held the first definite note of enquiry since he had come home.

He did not turn from the window.

'Not only mixing. Thinking as well,' he said.

Still he did not turn and face her, and a little dully Lady Hayley recognised the exact stance of her husband; the same stretch of neck, the same unwilling tone of voice. As if he were half expecting defeat and the sentence was therefore not worth completing. But John went on speaking.

'I came across a picture in one of my billets,' he said. 'You know, where those women are throwing themselves between the spears of the two armies. Now they *did* stop that war. Funny, isn't it? The picture was stained with damp. Hauled down from the attic, I suppose, to hide a bad patch of wallpaper. It's nothing to do with what we were talking about this morning, I know. But it set me off thinking along different lines, somehow. Instead of just accepting things like war and unemployment and all the rest I began to wonder *why*, and if it couldn't be prevented. Then I thought of you – '

'Well?' Lady Hayley's face wore the expression she used for particularly obstinate or stupid subordinates who failed to rally their districts to target level.

'Well,' he said, facing her at last, 'I know you wouldn't have done a thing like that – ' his mother made a gesture of impatience, 'and that there were hundreds like you, who called themselves leaders of the nation. *They* wouldn't either. They wouldn't try to stop a war, stop their men being killed. No! They wanted to be in on it. Organise it.'

'You don't know what you're saying, John. For one thing, women don't declare war. It's not their responsibility.'

'That's not fair,' he broke in. 'This morning you were saying that the people looked to you – to us. That's responsibility, isn't it? And surely it's time we led them into peace and security at home, rather than to death and poverty abroad?'

Lady Hayley made no further attempt to argue with her son; indeed, his statements were so wild and illogical, not to say utterly unfamiliar, that she could not follow them. Instead, she rose to her feet. 'Come into the oak room,' she said, 'I want to show you something.'

John turned from the window in surprise, then followed as she went from the room. Already he was regretting his words: he should have waited until these things were really clear in his mind. He knew from experience that however unassailable a conviction seemed when it was safe in his own head, directly he tried to express it he was lost in a confusion of words.

As they went through the door at the end of the silent hall he was wishing despairingly that he had thought more when days and weeks and years had been his as certainly as the clouds moved over the mountains. One spent so little time alone; looking back it was a lifetime of chatter. The army had made him remember every wasted minute of that former existence. Hours that could have been spent in the school – and later, the university – library. He thought with nostalgia of the polished perfection of the Bodleian. Austere tables and scholastic chairs, the ranged books; so much clear and penetrating thought between covers, evidence of quiet minds in slow-paced centuries.

They were in the oak room now, and he noticed that his mother was standing in the middle of the floor, waiting for him. It was a long, large room, entirely panelled in oak, with an old well-trodden oaken floor. The windows on one side reached down to within a foot or two of the floor and beneath their sill ran a polished hollow window seat. As a child John had kept his odd small treasures in it. Now it was quite empty;

he had looked when he first came home. The light that came through these tall windows made the room an effective gallery for the ranged family portraits. Beneath these were ancient weapons such as were usually found in the homes of peace-loving English gentlemen – curious intricacies of seventeenth-century Italian craftmanship, sheathed scimitars, swordsticks, old heavy pistols; and crisscrossing one corner, two red-tasselled halberds.

But Lady Hayley was pointing to the portrait of a grave and shadowed man.

'Your grandfather,' she said.

'Very bad,' John commented, looking up. His hands were in his pockets. 'And if you don't mind my saying so, mother, I think they are all in extremely bad taste. For one thing the painters are worse than second-rate.' He gestured to another painting. 'Look at great-uncle Horace embracing that marble fountain as if it were the baronetcy he prayed for all his life. And anyway, why so many rose-arbours and stone seats? I think factory chimneys would be more in the family tradition, don't you? Don't forget what great-grandfather made out of the industrial revolution. We're still living on the interest today.'

Lady Hayley's face began slowly to take on a rather ugly expression. To the boy it was painful to see all charm twisted out of it. At the same time it gave him some satisfaction to know that this face was not known to many people – probably only to his father and himself.

'These are your ancestors,' she said. 'Your cheap remarks won't alter that fact.' She walked slowly round the walls and

81

paused before a portrait here and there – a man in heroic stance, a woman serenely resigned to wealth. 'These relations of yours, at least a good many of them, died for their country. Died for *you*. They made England what she is. It is your duty to carry on that tradition.'

'I didn't ask them to bequeath me their tradition,' said John, 'I don't like it.' An old, submerged obstinacy was stirring in his voice. 'I wasn't born then, so how were they fighting for me? You mean they fought for an idea handed down to them; for their own position. Then they fought for *you*, for grandmother and great-aunt Anne; they had to fight, it was expected of them. Well, grandmother and great-aunt Anne are dead now, so what's the odds? They're all dead.'

'Dead, yes, they're dead!' cried his mother in a suddenly vibrant voice. 'We all die. I know that. And yet they live in the very air you breathe! They have passed on their tradition to you –'

'Tradition again! What is it exactly? An obligation to lead the people continually into war? Quote time-honoured clichés at them? Glory, honour? Dust is more glorious!'

'Oh, you are too unutterably callous, John! I can't – no, I can't talk to you.' For a moment Lady Hayley stood and gazed at the walls while the evening sun crept round the house and suddenly spilt into the room, making every metalled object dart tiny fires. In that moment her son looked at her with immense pain, for in her dignity and belief she *was* the past generation. He began to speak, to try once more to explain, but he was alone and the sound of his mother's low-heeled shoes came clopping back in echoes as she walked away from him down the hall, away and back to her patience.

* * *

After that his leave passed swiftly. Lady Hayley went to her meetings, and her son bicycled and fished, visited the Laceys and other neighbours, and one afternoon even went for a walk with his mother – each preserving the polite impersonality of a confirmed difference. Sometimes before going to bed he lingered in the shadow of the stable door, the day's defences down, heartsick for the soft blown breath of Owen Glyndwyr in the darkness, the intimate rustle of straw. He began to long for the army, his new life.

On his last day a letter came for him. It was from a friend of his, a man in his own Company. He was in London on twenty-four hours' leave, and suggested that John come up and join him. 'Let's meet in the Long Bar for lunch,' he wrote, 'we'll have a jolly good bust to finish off, old boy. Once back we don't know what they've got in store for us – or do we?' John handed the letter across to his mother; they were finishing breakfast.

'But on your last day!' she exclaimed. 'Surely – ' But at the expression on his face she stopped. 'You want to go up, don't you?' she asked.

He nodded quite briefly, already thinking of train connections. Could he make it?

'But the early local has gone,' said Lady Hayley, watching him with a flicker of emotion stirring her face. 'It connects with the fast London train, you remember – ' She glanced at her watch, ' – the next one isn't until this afternoon, and then from Dempsey to London it stops at every station.'

'But the express from Dempsey doesn't leave until ten-twenty,' John said, 'don't you remember the wait we always had on that chilly station? I've got an hour – I'll just do it if I take the car. Will that be all right?' He half rose, his mind racing ahead, his mouth dry with the dread of obstacles.

His mother almost flinched. 'Take the car on an unnecessary journey! I should think not . . . and who would drive it back from Dempsey?'

He paused at the door, bewildered; catching at the last part of her sentence. 'Who – but you, of course – '

His mother shook her head. 'You have made this sudden plan, John. What about *my* plans? I have kept this afternoon and evening free on account of it being your last day, and now – '

'But it's too late!' If he had not shouted the words he would have sobbed them. 'Too late, mother! – you're so busy ministering to the needs of a thousand unknown men that you forget the one who's here. *I'm* the reality, but you won't see it, won't believe it . . . you've got the energy of the heartless.' He was trembling, aware of the seconds passing, but powerless to go until he had spoken, until the bitter unhappiness had poured itself out in revenge. 'I shall take the car. It's the only damned bit of leave I've got left to enjoy and you're not going to spoil it!'

He raced upstairs (knowing it was not only himself, John Hayley, aged twenty, who had spoken; it was John Hayley the baby, the child, the schoolboy, the adolescent) and threw his things together. No time for goodbyes, that was just as well. He was leaving more than the house behind him this time.

To his surprise he did not find his mother guarding the garage doors. He wondered where she was as he got into the car and checked up on petrol; just enough and a bit over to get him the twelve miles into Dempsey. As he backed out of the garage he saw nothing before him but the crowd in the Long Bar, the queer folded positions people got into as they leaned on the counter and drank. He looked ahead to the gates and saw they were open – that would save a minute or two, anyway. He noticed that the rhododendrons were now in full flower, soon they would shrink and fall off, lie in heaps on the gravel.

Then he realised why the gates were open. His mother was ahead of him on her bicycle. He watched her with no trace of the red devouring rage of ten minutes ago. Now his mind was clear, he felt almost happy: he wanted to sing. Doggedly her blue uniformed figure pedalled and pedalled, and she looked dumpier than ever; solid and somehow impressive. But it was a stranger cycling, someone with a purpose alien to his own. He slowed down as he approached her, let down the window and called to her. But she did not turn her head, nor move her hands from the firm hold she had on the handlebars. He accelerated, raising dust; and was speeding past her. He listened for her voice, but only air rushed in through the window. Thoughtfully he wound the window shut again.

Soon Lady Hayley could see her car no longer. On and on she went, methodical and untiring, wondering why she had not opposed him – it would have been easy to lock up the garage – yet knowing that unlike his father, unlike *himself*, this time he would not have given in. She could imagine him smashing the locks with his gun. Heartless, that was what he had called her. Heartless, it seared up at her from his incoherence; familiar because it was an old accusation, one she could never understand. Her husband and her son, why had they always impeded her? Of course, her husband had been a failure, and failures were always touchy and arrogant, humble and admiring in turn. John was the same, although too young to be a confirmed failure yet. She smiled a little, with relief. Turning up the lane to the village hall, she thought, 'Of course he will write, say he's sorry. I shall keep all his letters . . .'

She found the women assembled, shook hands with some of them, smiled at the others. She had come to judge war-time recipes: cakes, puddings, biscuits, all containing some measure of soya flour. Miss Pollett, whose idea this was, led her round the entries. 'When does your son go back?' she asked, as they walked together to the platform.

'Today, this morning,' replied Lady Hayley.

Miss Pollett's eyes widened. 'And you found time to come – oh, Lady Hayley, you're *too* good!' Enthusiastic as was her tone, it flattened strangely into doubt.

After the prizes had been distributed, Lady Hayley spoke of the honour they had done her in asking her to judge the entries. She emphasised the need for the solidarity of women – it would be needed even more after the war, with all the men coming back, changed and strange to the forgotten ways of peace. War, she said, tested a woman even more than a man. A man, after all, had only one way before him, it was only a question of acceptance. A woman had to add to her usual roles of companion and mother, that of organiser. Naturally this involved sacrifices, loss and pain. It was a struggle all the time, with no medals at the end.

Just before she stepped down from the platform, she clasped her white-gloved hands and said, 'Do you know, more than ever I feel so much – so much at *one* with you all.'

Mechanically Miss Pollett smiled and found herself wishing with all her heart that Lady Hayley really meant it.

TO TEA WITH THE COLONEL

□□□□□□□

Miss Morton hated market day. It made her feel more than ever homeless, an outsider to these jostling voluble women who clotted the entrance to the many chemists and queued for cakes outside the most promising shops. On Wednesdays, borne to this border town in an overcrowded country bus, she felt stiffer and more apart than ever. If she succeeded in getting a seat early on in the eight-mile journey, she suffered from watching other women stand. At each grinding halt and the driver's unchanging and good-humoured 'Squeeze up a bit, there's good girls. One more aboard!' she would peer round the baskets piled with seasonable vegetables or fruit or flowers destined to be sold in the market, to see if the person getting on deserved her seat. At one stop in particular she dreaded the appearance of a thin little old woman who always got off at what she called the 'Orthopaedic', although Miss Morton could never see any signs of a clinic near the bus stop. When she first began to make these weekly shopping visits Miss Morton had always given up her seat, but now she suspected that the frail look of the old lady hid an indomitable good health and wiry will to live.

'She cannot possibly get as tired as I do,' she would murmur to herself as she stood in the packed heat of the bus, with other people's conversation and subtle, denigratory comments eddying round her head, 'if only they would open a window.'

On this particular Wednesday she had not stood, and the woman next to her, as if divining the curious torment she was suffering as she tenaciously clasped the strong leather shopping bag, rose ostentatiously as a young girl with a heavy baby lurched up the crowded aisle. Miss Morton kept her face away all through the journey, staring into the steamy window and mechanically wiping a neat oval spyhole to release her from the obvious friendliness of the young girl. As she looked out at the ploughed land, black as the rooks that flew heavily above the red hawthorn hedges, she wished fiercely for London: the blessed anonymity of a London bus.

Later, as she handed over her ration book and suffered the usual nausea at the caressing way the boy cut bacon – pawing it with an adolescent's thick ungraceful hands – she would have given anything, everything, to be back in Westbourne Grove in the littered cut-price shop where she was known and where the old man knew how difficult it was to live on rations for one.

'Shall I pack them up for you, Miss Morton?' The boy was leaning towards her, his voice lowered. 'We've some cake in today if you want it.'

To her surprise Miss Morton found herself blushing. She was inexplicably cheered. From her thin height she smiled at the boy, nodding. This was a courtesy she had not known in London, even in Westbourne Grove. The old man had invariably left her purchases scattered on the counter, then gone off with her money to shout for tea up the wooden staircase at the back of the shop. Perhaps then, as you became known, even here miles upon miles away from the shattered and shabby familiarities of your own streets, there was warmth and friendliness.

But even as the boy began to pack away the goods, she felt the constricting indecision upon her again. Should she tip him or not? Human relationships were so delicate, soured by a wrong word, an unwary gesture. Now he was handing her the bag across the counter, together with the change. She hesitated, seeing a sixpence ready, and then remembered that of course Christmas was near. Smiling uncertainly, she went out. The boy shrugged as he stared after her. 'Funny old girl,' he said to the pert young woman cutting up butter, 'wonder why she limps? There, d'you see?' They stared together now, craning over the bacon-slicing machine, but Miss Morton was lost among a surge of farmers coming from The Boar and heading for The Red Fox.

Not having to queue for cake, she went with relief into a small tea-room for coffee. This was one of the compensations of a Wednesday, and as she broke the home-made ginger biscuit she wondered whether she would perhaps go to the pictures and catch a later bus home.

'Ah, Miss Morton!'

The voice enfolded her in its eagerness and charm. It accompanied the noise of a scraping chair. The room was so small that to sit down at any of the precarious tables was a feat.

Miss Morton looked up to see a woman much younger than herself, dressed in sensible navy blue and bearing the same sort of bulging bag as she did. It was Miss Lumley from the Hall. She lived in the big deserted house with her father, Colonel Lumley, who was reputed to be over eighty and stone deaf.

The two women had often nodded greetings to each other during the nine months or so Miss Morton had lived in her small furnished cottage. But Miss Morton had often mentioned Miss Lumley in letters to her half-brother George, who had made it possible for her to go away when the ceiling came down on to the blue carpet of her Bayswater room. She had told him that the empty house could be filled with the uprooted people who drifted in, then out, of the remote Welsh village. In reply he had sent her his copy of the socialist weekly that carried a letter from him on that subject. Every week he sent this paper, telling her triumphantly that now perhaps she would believe him and join the Party.

But gazing across at the frank and likeable face of the Colonel's daughter, Miss Morton felt an obscure sense of guilt. George had said that such people made wars, then tried to get out of the responsibility a war created . . .

'How do you like it down here after London?' Miss Lumley was asking, before she screwed her head round to attract a waitress. 'Dull, I expect.'

Miss Morton murmured a phrase in reply.

'But the country people are really more friendly than townsfolk, don't you think?'

'Perhaps,' said Miss Morton, 'Maybe when you get to know them.'

Miss Lumley had now succeeded in giving her order, and for the first time looked at her companion.

'I hear you were bombed out,' she said, 'I'm so sorry – we don't realise it down here, of course – so far away. It must have been dreadful – '

'It was,' interrupted Miss Morton; she felt suddenly heroic. She wanted to talk, 'It isn't pleasant after four years of raids – you know you begin to feel a queer kind of invulnerability as time goes on – to wake suddenly with no warning and hear something crashing into your room. Or to reach for the lamp by your bed and find then that you can't move your legs. And to see what should be outside on the roof – tiles and things, you know – ' she gestured vaguely ' – piled on your bedspread and over your carpet, your chairs, your – '

The waitress brought coffee and biscuits.

'I suppose not,' said Miss Lumley. She looked uncomfortable, almost hurt. Weren't Londoners supposed to be like the R.A.F.? Not mentioning things like actual death and mutilation. Of course it was to be expected that a near-miss should make people voluble. The relief, of course. *Another second, and . . .*

'How dreadful for you,' she said.

After that they met often, and when they met they talked. Of the Red Cross, of the frequent gales that swept over the hills and down into the valley, of the skies which were different from peace-time; all the important trivia of country living.

There was between them a certain restraint, perhaps because of their growing sense of something shared; something they were not prepared to acknowledge. A diffidence towards other people, a submerged sardonicism. But gradually, as the weeks carried them forward from the wet winds of late autumn to the wet winds of a new year it became the custom for Miss Lumley to pick up Miss Morton whenever she had enough petrol to allow her to go into the nearest really big town for a Red Cross meeting. People saw them together – one tall and greying, with fierce deep eyes; the other more comely, younger, but already with the mark of spinsterdom upon her. To the countryside Miss Lumley was always 'Miss Kate.' She had taught in Sunday School, taken Brownies and Girl Guides and led the village activities since her mother's death. She was one of the dying race of acknowledged 'gentlefolk'. It would be a shock to the country people to see her marry.

As they walked back to the small, battered car together one day, Miss Lumley said: 'You've never met the Colonel, have you?'

Miss Morton was for a moment taken aback. The Colonel never went out. His life passed in unseen imperiousness within the walled garden and the empty house.

'No, I haven't,' she replied.

Miss Lumley said nothing more until they were in the car and edging out of the town, observing the Americans lounging wherever there was a wall to support their yearning backs. They exchanged slight, half-distressed glances, neither passing any comment.

'I wonder,' said Miss Lumley, as they cleared the welter of small streets that marked the finish or beginning of the town, 'I wonder if you would do something for me on Friday?' She half-laughed, and went on in a rush, 'You see, I've a tremendously important meeting at S——,' she named a place Miss Morton had never heard of, '– and even if I leave early in the morning I can't possibly be back until six-thirty.' She looked directly at her companion and asked, 'Would you give the Colonel his tea?'

Instantly Miss Morton thought of George and the socialist weekly. Tea with the Colonel! *You must have some principles, my dear Caro,* George seemed to be saying. His face would be screwed up in reluctant acknowledgment of the humour implicit in the frivolity of that unsuitable name. He distrusted humour, it might undermine the Revolution. *The People like a good belly-laugh with no frills.*

'I'd be so very obliged if you could manage it,' another, more charming, voice was saying.

'Why, of course,' said Miss Morton, 'I shall be pleased to.'

Miss Lumley explained that the daily woman left at three o'clock. She would leave everything ready. Could she arrive about quarter past four? The Colonel liked his tea at four-thirty to the minute.

As they parted at the cottage gate, Miss Lumley said, above the running engine, 'We don't use the front door now, the bell is out of order. You'll see the side door – it's through the shrubbery. So good of you. Four-fifteen, then.' She waved goodbye, then suddenly called Miss Morton back. 'Hadn't you better come up a day before? I'd forgotten. You've never been in the house. I must show you where the drawing room is.'

The next day Miss Morton went up to the Hall. On the way she posted a letter, telling herself that she was just dropping in on the way to the letter-box. As she went up the gravelled drive, which curved round the blind bulk of the house, she fought back the feeling that she was going to be interviewed for another job. '*Those days are over*,' she told herself, '*thanks to George*,' and made her way to the side door. It opened on to a stone wall of a yard and facing her was another door. This led directly into the house and she glimpsed Miss Lumley through the window, peeling potatoes at the sink. At the sight she was cheered, and when they greeted each other it was as if they were schoolgirls meeting without the sanction of their parents.

The small kitchen led into a much larger one, which could be, and evidently was, used as an occasional sitting-room. An open fire, with an oven above, was bright in the grate and tent poles and other camping equipment stood in one corner. There was an easy chair with a creased cretonne cover, and some cream coloured knitting on the seat. Miss Morton noticed all this with a queer nostalgic hunger; she had not stood in a proper kitchen for years. It was a luxury to walk from this one into the long passage that led to the front of the house, glimpsing spacious pantries on the way. She had almost forgotten that people had kitchens; living in one room a wall-cupboard served the purpose and was glamorised by the name of 'American Flatlet.' As for pantries . . .

Miss Lumley was hurrying ahead of her now, down a long corridor that changed into an oaken hall once past a heavy door that looked sound-proof. Here everything was quiet except for the uncertain sonority of a large-faced clock. Miss Lumley opened the drawing room door.

'I shall set this small table by the window if it is a fine day,' she was saying, 'but of course if it should happen to rain . . . no, it won't rain.' But Miss Morton scarcely heard her. She was looking out of the bay windows, looking across sloping lawns to the river and the hills beyond. An exclusive view, a private view. How right George was. To think of one family owning that enchanting curve of river!

Later on, back in her small cottage – one up, one down, and a dark cave of a scullery – she sat and wrote to George. When the letter was finished she went up to bed. Arriving here, she had revelled in going up her own stairs to bed; stairs she need share with no one else, no greetings to call out if she did not feel talkative. Sometimes it had been lonely and if she could have found the fare to London without going to the village post office and drawing on her savings, she would have done so. But she had conquered loneliness here as well as in London. Here you could keep a cat, two cats, without a landlady sniffing suspiciously as she came into the room. Here, although your neighbours carried on conversation across a hundred yards or so of garden, hedge and lane, they did not stamp or pull heavy chairs across your ceiling. And their laughter was different from town laughter.

On Friday, at a quarter past four, Miss Morton again walked up the drive to the Hall. At the sight of the prepared teatray on the kitchen table, the small plates of sandwiches and square brown cakes, all carefully covered with a table napkin, she sensed the importance of the Colonel's tea at four-thirty. Slipping off her coat, she set the kettle on to boil. Then she stepped back, the thick silence of the house making her move clumsily, so that she knocked her bad leg against a chair. The pain was so sharp and unexpected that she was thrown into an unreasoning rage. It was so unfair – surely her life had been unfruitful and difficult enough without this added burden. As she sat nursing the scarcely-healed shin – the bone had been cracked that night when the sky toppled into her room – almost crooning over it, all her latent hatred revived. Hatred for people who had never known the nightly horror of sirens. But *he* wouldn't have heard them anyway. Funny to think that someone in England had never heard that sound. When she first came down here, there had been periodic try-outs in the market town, and she remembered wishing fiercely that real death-planes would fly over the uncaring people and bomb them into realisation. But the mood had quickly passed; you could not these days wish destruction on anyone, except of course your enemies. George said you could, but then George had been through it all, was living now up there among the old havoc. Perhaps he would change, hate *her* soon.

To defeat the coldness that this feeling brought her, she opened the door and went into the hall. She stood still, looking up the shallow oaken staircase. To think those two lived here alone, and all these rooms! She found herself reckoning up how many people could be contained in the house. Say one or two to a room, roughly fifteen rooms, judging by the windows, that was . . . But a door down the corridor was opening, and the sound was so stealthy, so soft and unobtrusive in the breathing silence that she jumped. Then, as if to point the action, the grandfather clock near her wheezed in preparation for the half-hourly salute. It demolished time, she thought, with an odd stab of fear and perception. When the house was gone it would be somewhere, in a saleroom, perhaps, still beating out the centuries. But the Colonel was on his way to the drawing room and Miss Morton, feeling the ghost of a parlour-maid's panic, hurried back to the kitchen to make tea.

As she went into the drawing room she saw the Colonel seated at the table, his hands gravely folded and a thick stick by his side. He rose and nodded, without smiling. Then he sat down again. A tiny spurt of tea came from the spout on to the lace cloth and Miss Morton saw his face contract, but he still said nothing. But he was watching her as she sat down, and passing his cup, she felt he knew she had put on her best silk dress for the occasion. He became absorbed in the sandwiches almost at once, and then she could look at him. A surprising man for eighty, small and slight, with an obstinate uprightness and hard schoolboy colour that shouldered aside the years as impatiently as, a decade ago, his horse must have cleared the road of villagers.

'He is thinking I am a "neat little body,"' thought Miss Morton with sudden fury. Quite respectable enough to sit opposite him and hand him a cup of tea.

Then the emptiness of the house, of the whole countryside at this poised hour was borne in on her by a flurry of ducks somewhere out of sight of the window. She and the Colonel were alone. Realising this, she smiled so swiftly that it was gone in an instant; then she spoke, glancing around the room as she did so.

'When I think of the numbers of people your family have kept poor in order to build this house, I want to wreck it all – ' Her teeth were gritted as she gestured towards the garden.

The Colonel looked once at her, and after a moment's hesitation, nodded. Then he went on with his tea; his movements were those of the very old, persistent but unforceful. Miss Morton wondered for a sickening instant whether he could lip-read, but decided against it, for he was not the sort of man to take the trouble. Also, she reasoned, with her new and suddenly unmuddled mind, that at his age and the kind of life he had led, he would have no interest in what others had to say to him. They had said it all before: in childhood, in youth and in middle age. All the words he had ever wanted to hear had been spoken long ago.

Fighting down her release, her exhilaration, Miss Morton's eyes caught those painted in a portrait hanging at the further end of the room. She was amazed at herself; her words seemed to be addressed to all those who had ever slighted or hurt her. Nodding towards the picture with a smile, she said, 'I expect that old rogue was your father. Turning people out of their farms to put his own family in. A bad landlord, I'll be bound. Yes, there's a definite likeness.'

The Colonel caught her gesture and followed her gaze.

'My father,' he said briefly, in the soft, tentative voice of the deaf.

Miss Morton felt something perilous as a giggle start in her stomach and could not control a slow smile that on a face less thin and dark would have been a grin. So it was as easy as this to humiliate the powerful and the wealthy! She offered the Colonel a cake and he took it. He hesitated whilst she poured another cup of tea for him, then spoke:

'I see you have been admiring the garden. It is the only piece of land that is left. Everything else is sold. The times.' He smiled almost painfully, and lifted a hand as he saw Miss Morton's mouth opening to answer him. He looked at her with his bright blue eyes and went on. 'I do appreciate your giving me tea, Miss Morton. But surely my daughter warned you that normal conversation is out of the question for me? I cannot hear any of the charming things you have been saying to me.' He bowed his head a little. 'It is my loss.' And he turned his eyes to his plate again.

For a moment Miss Morton sat utterly still. It was as if someone had lifted a weight of pain and degradation from her years of living nervously in rooms, of odd jobs that meant just enough food: hurrying, graceless crowds. Then, quite suddenly, she burst into tears.

The Colonel would have spoken, but he was no longer in contact with the world. And he had never known what it was to doubt or bitterly regret a cruelty, for he had never been cruel. So he stood, concerned and helpless, while the sun flooded into the room, giving it the grace, polish and serenity of a discarded age.

THE NOTEBOOKS

🀫🀫🀫🀫🀫🀫🀫

It was only after her husband's death that Mrs. Roughton began to sleep in the afternoons. It was peculiarly fitting, she thought, voluntarily to withdraw from the brightness of the day, to pull the curtains upon it and lie flat on one's back beneath an eiderdown. From that position, twisting silk-stockinged toes together, she could see how the contours of the room altered, how dominating was the wide bulging chimney which took up so much space in the bedroom of this old house. It grew up from the room below, through the floor and then on up through the invisible beams of the roof, to emerge with its smoky plume of woodsmoke above the tiles.

It was hard at first to sleep in the heart of the day, she was so unaccustomed to it. The afternoons had been her most active time. She and Lenny had gone out for long bicycle rides together up and down the persistent hills of this border country. Or else they walked over to a familiar slope where a dead tree menaced the countryside with its witches' fingers, and Lenny wove fantastic tales around it. But that was over; now Mrs. Roughton slept. She was determined to do so, and although she woke dazed and dry-mouthed from her unnecessary and reluctant dozing, it was always with some satisfaction that she noted the time was after four and she could have tea.

The evenings she spent going over Lenny's manuscripts and answering any letters there might be. He was still getting requests for work, she noticed. Did these people not know he was dead? Or perhaps they hoped to gain notoriety by publishing posthumous stories. How often had he said that death was an indispensable part of fame.

There she went again! Why did his words hang so in the air? She must build up her life without him, although after fifteen years together it was a titanic task. They had never been in an intimate circle of friends, and always withdrew when too many people started dropping in. It had been a relief to get away to the country – in London, too many times had come the jocular yet implacable tap at window or door which prefaced an evening of talk. Why was it, Mrs. Roughton wondered now, sitting alone before her fire, that so many of them had the power to drain us? Maybe we were solidly fixed, they always knew that whatever divorces, scandals or rows went on, we endured together. They must have felt the need for our stability, we gave them a sort of strength.

She made up the fire, quickly and nervously. I've no strength to give away now. She pulled out a book from a circular bookcase by her side but it was impossible even to start it. The words were isolated, had no meaning when strung together. 'I've never knitted,' she said aloud, aggressively. 'Perhaps I'd better learn. That or patience.' But instead, she settled back in her chair, all her energy going the forbidden way of regrets. We had planned such a lot of things for after the

war, I can't believe . . . but it was true, the emptiness in the
room testified to it. It was true that Lenny was no longer a
physical presence in worn trousers and check coat. The door
would never again open to admit him as it had done that chill
spring day not three months ago; his finger held up comically,
as if to minimise the pain of a torn nail got by a slip on the hill-
path up to their house. She had jumped up then in concern
to bring hot water and salt (they had no disinfectant in the
house – a rare thing this – and salt was said to be just as good,
dissolved, a large tablespoonful of it). She had bound the
finger up for him and they had forgotten it by bedtime. In the
morning he had said tentatively, half-fearing her disbelieving
smile, that it was throbbing badly. She had insisted on his going
to the doctor. Remembering, this one thought took the
edge slightly off her pain. The doctor had dressed the finger,
dismissed any possibility of further developments and told him
in an offhand way to come back the next day if the throbbing
started again. The next day the finger swelled, and by night-
time Lenny complained of a pain in his armpit. They both
thought the pain was the outcome of his dread, pure
imagination, so after plunging the finger into hot water and
proper disinfectant (she had bought some by this time), and
soaking it in iodine, they did not go to the doctor until the
following day. She met the district nurse in the village and told
her about it. 'He fell?' said the nurse, 'On that path up the hill?
Oh yes, it is gritty, isn't it? Did the doctor give him an injection
of any sort?' Mrs. Roughton had known then that this worse
than no-action on the part of a testy, over-worked country
doctor was going to wreck their lives. Her inside went cold.

She had known it by the urgency with which the nurse had bundled her into the little car and driven straight home. They found Lenny upstairs, in front of a mirror, vainly trying to get his jaws apart. He made a slight noise as they came to him and she remembered his eyes. He was trembling, and a desperate fore-knowledge was in the look he gave her, although on the way to the doctor it was he who held her hand tight, as if it were she who was suffering, would suffer . . .

At the doctor's the nurse phoned for an ambulance. By lunch-time they were at the hospital.

All that day she sat by him, watching the needle being pricked into his arm, filling him with the serum that, three days ago, would have saved him. They flooded him with it, fed him meanwhile with fluid piped through a gap in his teeth. His muffled, difficult voice spoke to her, 'Lucky that tooth got knocked out, eh, old girl?' For himself he seemed to have discovered an attitude; once in the middle of a situation that strangely enough had haunted him since boyhood, he was quiescent. By dawn the next day his jaws relaxed, the injections had beaten the germ. They sent her off to sleep, saying he would be all right now. But as if life seemed determined to be done with him, he developed pneumonia through shock. All the next day and the day after he fought this new evil. He was nearly through the fever when his heart, always unpredictable, refused to co-operate with the mind trying to drive it over the peaks of fever. It stopped. Yes, at six-thirty in the evening, with the fever subsiding, the finger down to normal, and nurses drawing the long blue curtains over the dusky windows, Lenny died. It was so sudden, so unexpected, that even the young hospital doctor was shocked out of his professional acceptance of death. He took it as a personal affront, and swore under his breath at the weak heart which had so subtly betrayed them all. Then with a short, wry look at Mrs. Roughton, he covered Lenny's face.

There had been a post-mortem. Sitting before her fire with cold hands Mrs. Roughton thought of a dozen shattering things she could have said, but hadn't. The local doctor himself was not present, a colleague deputised for him. Was it medical etiquette only which made him swear there had been no negligence? It was impossible to get the anti-tetanus serum, he declared, it would have meant a twelve-mile drive. A doctor could not, in wartime, inject everyone who happened to cut his hand. Labourers were continually scratching their hands on the hedgerows, grazing them in the fields, cutting them at harvest time. They were surrounded by soil and yet no harm ever came of it. How was his distinguished colleague to know this was to be one case in a thousand?

So it was death by misadventure, nobody censured. And Mrs. Roughton felt the reproach of the court on her. There were men still dying in battle, and here was she making a fuss about the death of a man who had taken no active part in that battle. A civilian. A man who wrote books for a living.

To stop the endless retrospective questioning, the recurrence of hysteria that made her want to destroy the doctor, the coroner and everyone else who had taken part, Mrs. Roughton went to her husband's desk. In the bottom drawer she found the heavy blue books she had forgotten in the turmoil of the aftermath. What a hum of activity surrounds the coming into life and the going from it! But, she told herself wryly, where would we be without a little ceremony to help us? Howling like savages, stamping our mad despair and ignorance round a campfire. Holding the books close to her, she wondered for a moment whether the civilised way of letting grief trickle out in regulated channels was, after all, the best thing. One wild frenzy of terrible, abandoned rage at the unfairness and inevitability of the ways of the universe . . . but she had been over it all with herself before. She put the books on the table.

These were Lenny's notebooks. From their earliest, grimiest days together she remembered him bending over them; sticking in newspaper cuttings that might inspire in a dull patch, copying passages from authors he admired or notes from his smaller, pocket-size notebooks. And through them all the absentminded caricatures and sketches. It was at these she looked now, recognising an evil-seeming bus conductor who had been insulting when they went to the front seat at the top of an empty bus on an expedition to Kew Gardens. A woman with the dessicated, used face of a street-walker. Then, turning at random, unexpected sketches of herself asleep. Men of all sorts, large heads on dwindling bodies. All done with few lines and an instinctive grasp of what lay behind the convenient mask of the moment. That same keenness had informed his writing. She would say to him, half in exasperation: 'I'm sure you don't really see what's going on. Look at you, you're walking in a dream!' But even as she spoke Lenny was eliminating the surface wash of the street; the shop windows, the tiring passage of buses and girls, old men tapping along, eternal kerbstones. And arriving back in their rooms he would say, 'Did you notice that old woman in the tea place? She's been round here for years, looks as if she's strayed from an eighteenth-century vignette. How carefully she lives, always that glass of milk . . . I expect her nurse told her once that it would make her grow, so now she believes it will keep her alive.' Then his expression would change, and she knew he was pained at the idea of so many greying people who had outlived both their times and their friends, living on tenaciously in their single rooms and paying coins into slots for their baths, their light, their warmth. Going from the nearest ABC to the gardens to sit in the free heat of the sun, carefully stepping on to buses for the meagre journeys they undertook.

I never noticed people in that way, Mrs. Roughton acknowledged now, her hand straying in late pity over the stiff pages of the book. I was taking in too much of the coming and going and it always left me with a headache. You can only *see* people if you relax and forget yourself.

Suddenly the silence of the room seemed tangible; it lay like the first surface of dust on a polished chest, or the imperceptible skinning-over of her life. In almost clumsy haste she went to the radio, turned the knob at random and heard a throbbing beat of men marching and whistling. In a second the room was full of it, the whistling had given way to a subdued chorus and she felt her own foot caught in the rhythm,

My Lili of the Lamplight
My own Lili Marlene

And the tramp tramp of marching men grew fainter and fainter until the suave voice of a band leader announcing the next item, a novelty number, made her laugh shakily at the tears that were making her head feel big and full. To weep at twenty men sitting round a microphone stamping their patent-leathered feet! But no, it was the song itself that went marching on in her head, in step with her own private grief. Snatched as it had been from the airways of the enemy, it embodied the giant despair and nostalgia of men and women divided, of the inevitability of that separation. The lamplight could be on East Side or Tottenham Court Road, Boulevard Rochechouart or any Marktplatz. Human beings, Mrs. Roughton found herself thinking, have so much in common: hate as well as love, venom as well as kindliness. With sorrow the common denominator of them all. She sighed slightly, a breath-caught sound, and went to the mirror to speak to the face she saw there. 'I'm only thirty-six,' she said. 'I shall go back to London, look up a few of our friends . . . ' but what about money? Lenny had always seen to that. They had never thought much about it and yet there had always been enough for their needs of the moment. There would be royalties from time to time, of course, and she might get some kind of job.

There was a sudden ring at the door, and turning off the radio Mrs. Roughton hurried to open it. She was alarmed and puzzled, and did not know the man who stood outside. It was a shock to see him, she felt hurt and oddly put out at this fresh reminder of the number of men in the world who in no way resembled Lenny.

'I'm sorry to call on you so late,' the stranger began, 'But I'm on my way back to Branstead, and I was passing . . . you *are* Mrs. Roughton – '

'Yes, won't you come in?' she said.

'I'm sorry to call on you so late,' he repeated, following her into the small room off the hall. 'My name is Parks, Ronald Parks. I am director of the Branstead Museum, and I wondered – '

'Please sit down,' she interrupted. 'Now, I'm sure I've heard your name.'

'Yes, I was speaking to your husband – oh, and I would like to offer you my – '

'Thank you,' Mrs. Roughton accepted the unfinished regrets with a repudiatory gesture, and Mr. Parks pulled his earlobe as if he liked to hurt it, delicately, and went on; 'Well, Mrs. Roughton, your husband was considering selling the museum the original manuscript of his latest novel. He wrote his books by hand, I believe? They were typed afterwards?'

'Yes, that's quite right,' she replied. 'He never did any typing, he – '

'I offered him a hundred pounds for it,' said Mr. Parks modestly.

'You must think a great deal of his work, have you read all his books?'

He coughed in slight reproach. 'Well, no, Mrs. Roughton, I'm a busy man, you know, not much time – however, I've read one or two. And don't forget your husband was a Branstead boy. It's only right . . .'

'Of course,' she rose and went from the room to find the manuscript. How absurd, Lenny a Branstead boy, a sharp giggle caught her as she rummaged in the deep cupboard by the stairs. Quite a local-boy-makes-good touch. When she came back she saw Mr. Parks bending over the notebooks she had left open on the table. Instantly rage and near panic made her hurry across the room. He was chuckling.

'Remarkable,' he said, 'quite the caricaturist! Ah yes, dear me, what a talent.' He turned away reluctantly, stretching out his hand for the bundle of closely written papers she held. He pulled off a coloured garter that had enclosed them and handed it to her with an echo of gallantry. He flicked through with an intent, business-like alertness. Then he sat down and pulled out his cheque book. 'This is what I was after,' he said. 'One hundred pounds.' He sent a sudden shrewd glance up at her. 'I could make it two fifty with the notebooks.'

Mrs. Roughton's hands instinctively covered the heavy blue books that lay so perilously near the ready pen, the impeccable tweed arm.

'I'm sorry,' she said, in a breathless, almost frightened voice. 'No.'

He continued to gaze up at her blandly. 'Excuse my saying so, dear Mrs. Roughton,' he remonstrated gently, 'but aren't you being just a *little* bit selfish? Your husband had many admirers, you know. Think of the pleasure those other people would get from such intimate records as these books offer.'

'I don't care much about other people,' Mrs. Roughton's voice was suddenly high with anger. 'They will soon forget him. They were not married to him – how could they hope to know him? I won't have you buying up my life.'

Mr. Parks said nothing. When he had written the cheque he left it on the table and rose to go. At the door he merely said, 'I shall be waiting for you to change your mind. After all, it wouldn't be your husband's wish for you to shut yourself up and brood. Believe me, Mrs. Roughton, you would really be much happier if you got rid of all these – er – painful reminders.'

'Goodnight,' she said, shutting the door and quite forgetting that the path to the gate could only be sensed, not seen, in the heady darkness of an early May night. All the same, his words had made an impression on her; rather, they had awakened an attitude of mind that linked up with the days when, secure in love and life, she and Lenny had discussed the impossibility of one of them dying before the other. 'I should cut right away,' he had said, 'leave everything that remotely reminded me of you. Probably live the sort of life that people regard as loose and easy – but which is really the most exacting, as every debauchery has to be created first in the mind, then deliberately blanked out so that desire can be worked up and the whole thing gone through in the flesh.' He had laughed at the concern on her small and shockable face and pulled her nose gently. 'But that's not going to happen, my sweet one. If *I* die first and you marry again, I'll come and haunt you. That's fair warning!'

How tragically purposeful are the words of the dead remembered by the living. Now Mrs. Roughton thought that even the ghost of Lenny would be some comfort. But this made her angry with herself: it was a bad thing to feel that the two of them had become grafted into each other through the close association of years. It was a betrayal of oneself, of the individual essence that was poured into each one of us, so to depend on another human being. *When one limb is cut off another replaces its function.* The words leapt to her mind, reminder of an uncle waggling his maimed right hand at her to emphasise his point and to demonstrate how he held a pen between little finger and thumb, yet still wrote a good hand.

'I won't depend on him any more,' she said aloud to the silent room. The fire had gone down and it was chilly, 'I'll pack those books up and go to London.'

The next day, before she could change her mind, she sent off the notebooks to Mr. Parks. Then she wrote to a friend who had wanted to rent the small house for a few months of the summer in return for her own flat, and arranged the exchange. Everything went off flawlessly, Mr. Parks sent a cheque by return; he was delighted, he said she would never regret it.

Once in her friend's flat Mrs. Roughton tried to fit herself into a new rhythm of existence. She tried to telephone people they had known together, but each time her hand paused on the dial. She gave herself advice; 'You should see people, not stay moping by yourself.' That was the sort of advice the world gave, affronted by anyone who stayed apart or who moved among crowds with an unseeing face. She laughed a little at the easy way one said 'people', as if they were glued together, admirable as automatic grief-absorbers. There was another way, though; a way back into another time.

So one morning she found herself on a bus going through long shopping streets, through streets of houses, their little front gardens guarded by low stone walls and privet hedges. At last a small bridge, a public house facing the bus-stop, and opposite a long stretch of grass; she was here.

She started to walk up the road, which, one of many, had bounded her safe childhood and she glanced about alertly and felt elated. Apart from, and yet curiously bound up with, the shabbiness that lay everywhere like flood or storm wrack, was the sense of a lack of that mystery which had made certain houses, certain paths, so tremulously unexplorable. Glancing through a broken fence into a once-wealthy, completely private garden, she saw how vegetables had trespassed on to the smooth lawn; a man bulging out of a dressing gown was packing crates in a littered conservatory. From pinstriped mornings to pyjama-ed afternoons, thought Mrs. Roughton, only a six-year war could do that. Walking across the common she noticed paths across the grass worn by feet she would never know; noticed how much taller were the trees, how untidy the gorse and blackberry bushes. Now here were the shops – going in past improvised opaque windows and shabby doors, it was a shock to find new faces. Nobody remembered her, yet here, as a schoolgirl, she had chosen among the long shoelaces of licorice, the jelly-babies, the bright spurious cornets. Later, her copies of *Schoolgirl's Own* or *The Magnet* had been weekly events.

On her way back to the small station an elderly woman stopped her, then an old man. On the faces of each were looks of tardy recognition, then reproach and pain – not so much directed at her as at the relentless flow of the years that allowed a young girl to grow into the likeness of father or mother, and yet not wholly become either. Their eyes were lost to a past time. They were not interested in this shoddy present; where old friends lay under the granite chips of easily tended graves narrow as cradles, their alien children usurping the known places. And Mrs. Roughton, as an alien child, also felt in some way betrayed, finding pain in the aged and changing faces. These people who had made up the daily world of a child, were stanchions; inviolate. In her mind's eye she had often seen them doing the same things – cutting the lawn on Sunday mornings, sitting at tea in cool, polished rooms, picking cherries for her from their gardens, gravely processing to and from church to the sound of their own serene voices and lolloping evening bells.

After it all, she was left vacant, the wind blowing gusts of smoke past the carriage window on her way back to town, obscuring any last glimpses.

Another week passed, and then she decided to see the people she and Lenny had met together. At least they had known her in the more important, because self-chosen, phases of her life. But with them, despite their kindliness and welcome, she still missed Lenny, felt his lack acutely in discussions and found herself hesitating for a word that Lenny might provide. Once or twice, on arriving at somebody's house she hovered at the door, her eye going towards the clock, about to say, 'Hasn't he come yet? I'm so sorry, he's always late.' Or going home, would realise with a shock that there would be no one to fetch her, or to be at the other end, waiting.

One day, after six weeks of this determined living, she gave way to the recurring impulse to go down to Branstead Museum. Just to see the notebooks would be strengthening, she felt. It would, in some way, be a reaffirmation.

It was a warm summer day when she stepped off the train, a weak shakiness in her stomach as in the days when to meet Lenny was difficult, a rushed time. She took a bus to the museum, walked up the chill stone steps and through chill arches into a tiled space which must be called a *vestibule*. No one was about, and she went first into a large room on the right with stuffed birds, foxes and other unfortunate wild things, petrified, for the benefit of the citizens of Branstead, in a travesty of their normal swift grace. Then she went into a smaller room, where old broken tiles lay in glass cases, tabulated on white cards. Pottery, twisted copper implements, and all the other sordid, poignant leftovers of a past age. She laughed at the thought of carefully pompous magnates sealing up an "explanation of our times" to put beneath the foundation stone of a large new building. 'Who cares?' she asked herself in the high stone chill of the place, 'Atlantis was submerged, we shall be blown, literally, heaven high.'

She went, with a small frigid smile on her face, up more stone steps. No, that was the door to the public library. Avoid that, avoid all public libraries. But along the wall were some glass cases. Her smile gone, she went up to them. In one an ancient yellowed book – some previous Lord Mayor's household accounts. In another, examples of modern book-jackets. At the end, under glass, lay one of Lenny's notebooks.

She saw a poem he had cut from a newspaper and stuck in. Her eye went familiarly to the last verse:

> *I would think until I found*
> *Something I can never find.*
> *Something lying on the ground*
> *In the bottom of my mind.*

Then, to connect up with this, as if the healing words were spoken, not seen, those other few lines jumped at her:

> *If I were as wise as they*
> *I would stray apart and brood*
> *I would beat a hidden way . . .*

She did not see the rest of the open pages, did not regret that the book was locked away from her. The words were beating warmth into her mind and body: she had not realised how cold she had been for weeks, months.

'Of course, darling,' she said, her hands gentle on the glass top. 'It is right for your books to be here. You're an echo of warmth in this bitter place.'

Turning, she went again down the steps. She went slowly, accepting the fact that rooms would always remain empty for her, however many people filled them. Accepting the implicit challenge, the need to search for that something in the bottom of her mind.

CHANCE CALLERS

◻◻◻◻◻◻◻

He felt cold up there in the hills above the pine wood, and was surprised to see his wife take off her coat with a pleased sigh.

'First really warm day this year,' she said, 'let's sit down.'

Out of the blue he replied, settling himself on the coat beside her, 'Nice to be alone with you, even though it is only in a windy field.' She looked up at him sharply. He looked chilled, she said; she kept forgetting – should they walk on?

'No, sit still, sit still. I've had an overdose of solicitude.' He slipped an arm round her and gazed at the spring fields, the river curving slowly below and the purplish brush of twiggy trees that hid the village. Watching the day wheel by, he did not notice that she sat tightly against his arm, a stiffness of dissatisfaction in her attitude. It was one of those clear, sweeping days of early spring when the sky itself seems lifted higher by a blue wind; a day when instead of being filled with a thousand discontents, a man knows only one – his utter inadequacy before God.

Frank felt some of this piercing humility as he watched the first green crops darken to a cloud or shine to its passing. He could not speak.

'I can't expect you to like this part of the country, I know that,' his wife was saying, a sort of aggrieved logic in her voice. 'I suppose you've seen enough green to last you a good few years.' She had softened her body to his, letting herself rest more heavily on his shoulder. He looked down, startled. It had happened once or twice before during these few weeks, he remembered, her saying with such certainty the exact opposite of what he was thinking. It shifted the future out of perspective, made him doubt the present and envy the past. He resolved to find out exactly what sort of a man he had been three and a half years ago, and become like him – if only to preserve the dangerous present which melted so invisibly and inevitably into the future. But how could he recognise that slightly shabby, more or less contented figure, across such expanses of sea and mountain, jungle and swamp and prison camp? He had often dreamt of it, and the face had swum nearer from that far-off shore, then was gone again before he could catch it and look into its eyes.

'Oh, come on Frank. It's not so warm after all. Let's go this way.' To force him to speak, she pointed over the valley, towards a large white house, surrounded by sparse trees. Did he see? Captain Banks lived there. Fancy, twelve rooms and only he and his brother to live in them!

Her voice held such truculence that Frank suddenly felt it as a challenge. What she meant, perhaps, was 'twelve rooms and we can't get one, we've got to live with auntie in her tiny cottage.' Her eyes were on the house hungrily.

'That makes six rooms each,' he said, 'we could do with a couple, eh, old girl?'

Glancing down, he saw with satisfaction that he had spoken with the tongue of that other man. What pleased him better was that he had said the words without consciously framing them – they had come unbidden, easily. Maybe, then, with time, he could get back to what he had been, pick up the strands that bound him to this loyal, likeable woman who was his wife.

'But I thought you wanted to get back to town?' he asked curiously, wondering fleetingly if she too had changed. 'Said you were fed up with three years in the country with nothing to do but win the baking competitions at the Women's Institute.'

She smiled a little, fleetingly. She could not explain to him the real reason why to go back to the town where they had lived so briefly together would be dreadful to her, a sort of death. She did not quite know herself. The peeling, exhortatory posters, the queues, the prefabricated houses planted like sugar boxes amongst the cleared debris had something to do with it – but not all. In an effort to pin down a fraction of this feeling, she said, her face like a stone, 'I couldn't bear to live in our old street again. I'd be remembering the Verneys under all those bricks.'

His heart lifted to her, and he squeezed her arm. 'If I find you a house to live in here, in this valley, would you like it?'

She glanced at him in disbelief. She had all the assurance of her time away from him, an assurance built up first as a defence against the prickly hedge of dislike for evacuees, then slowly strengthened by tussles with 'The Labour' and tussles with 'them' at the War Office, who had wanted to stop her money when Frank was 'presumed dead'. So now it was out of her tough elasticity of spirit that she declared in all sincerity that if *she* had failed to find a place to live, what did he think he could do?

But Frank obviously had an idea. He was flushed, and he explained it to her as they swung downhill. She recoiled, shocked, pooh-poohed it; pressed his hand and said 'You are a devil, Frank. You haven't changed after all.' He was immensely cheered by this, and his excitement made him feel a little faint. He staggered a little, then had to sit down.

With a kind of exasperated tenderness his wife took his shoulders hard against her breast and held a small bottle in front of his nose. He sniffed obediently. Over the fumes she said, 'You get so *excited*,' looking at him long and anxiously.

He handed back the smelling salts without a word. The bitter fumes had certainly cleared his head. As if nothing had happened he suggested they walk on to the house and carry out his idea.

'Don't be absurd,' she said, glancing at him. 'You were only joking – we must get back for tea. You mustn't be out for too long. The doctor – '

'The doctor said I mustn't be crossed, didn't he? "Humour him, Mrs. Johnson, however silly his whim may appear to be. Don't forget he is still in a state of near neurosis . . ." He stopped his imitation when he saw the dismay on her face. 'Yes, I *was* listening,' he admitted in a lighter tone, wanting her to laugh. 'Come on now, Beryl, it's worth a try.'

Arm in arm they went across meadow lands boggy with the spring floods, round fields where winter wheat and barley showed an inch or two of green promise, then up a lane full of green honeysuckle and elder and early primroses and so to the gates of the drive. Here they both hesitated, the house was solid, set in its own ways, hostile to strangers. Beryl said, 'It's no use, Frank. He wouldn't even have anyone billeted on him. Come away, do.' But he seemed to gather fresh heart from her dissuasion, and pulled her after him up the drive.

The wide wooden porch had glass panels let into the sides and the sun came warmly on to them without the chilly wind to negate it. Frank straightened himself, seemed to expand. Beryl noticed that his face changed, growing fuller, making his scar less apparent. She had a way of watching him and checking up on the fleeting unknown expressions that crossed his face: one day she was sure she would know them all. The door opened before either of them had lifted the black sphinx-headed knocker.

'Good afternoon,' said Captain Banks.

They turned to him, startled, and noticed that he carried a gun loosely in one hand as if he were more often with it than without. He noticed what they were looking at. He told them in his even, courteous voice that he had been out shooting his owl's dinner. 'I found him when he was a baby,' he said, 'his wing was broken. It's healed now, but I still provide his food.'

He watched them steadily with his blue eyes. He had a large skull and a small face, but this effect may have been due to the hair receding almost to the top of his head. Although not excessively tall, he was an impressive man. His stained gaiters and worn boots, the leather jacket and high-necked grey pullover were badges of his standing in the county. No lesser man could wear them.

'Don't stand there on my doorstep,' he said a little sharply, 'you must have some reason to call, so come in and join me at tea.'

Demurring slightly, Beryl followed him across the dark polished hall to a small room on the right. Leaning his gun in a corner the Captain told them to sit down whilst he made some more tea.

They sat a little awkwardly on a large settee, half covered with a plaid travelling rug, on which lay a black spaniel. Frank felt oddly deflated. He had meant to issue his challenge on the doorstep; now, sitting in this sunny room waiting for tea to be handed him by a stranger, he floundered. When he spoke, his words came jerkily.

'We saw your house from the hill.'

The Captain seemed pleased. 'The house can be seen from almost any point on the hills,' he said. 'As children we were never lost.' He had put fresh tea in the pot and now took the steaming kettle from the fire, poured it in and stirred it a moment. 'Aren't you the young fellow Johnson all the fuss was about? Band at the station – flags, streamers and all the rest?' He turned to a cupboard and took two more cups and saucers from it. 'How did you like it?'

Frank looked apologetically at Beryl, but she was staring, fascinated, at the Captain. 'It was kind of them all,' he replied, 'but it rather shook me up, if you know what I mean. So much fuss – ' he took the proffered cup with an embarrassed laugh.

The Captain spun round and gave Beryl her tea. He passed her the sugar with an accusing stare. 'Stupid fools,' he said, 'the lot of 'em. I told them the boy'd be in no fit state for all that fa-di-da. You're his wife, I suppose? Well, you should have stopped 'em – nothing the people down here like better than an excuse to go mad. Makes 'em feel they were really in the war.' Calming down a little at the startled look on Beryl's face he turned again to Frank, telling him to sit down and drink his tea, for God's sake. Then he settled himself by the fire before shooting out another question. 'Three years prisoner of war, eh? That's no picnic. Where were you?'

'Siam,' said Frank, 'not too bad the first year or so. I was in a base camp for wounded, and the army patched me up before the Japs took the hospital. Then that confounded railway . . . yes, I've been darned lucky.' He glanced down, not wanting to see the look he had caught on so many faces – the horror, shock, awe at his survival; the furtive hope of first-hand information.

But Captain Banks almost ignored his words and began speaking to Beryl, asking her if she intended to return home now her husband was back.

As Beryl made to reply, there came a faint tapping from overhead. They all looked up, and Captain Banks left the room immediately with a muttered apology. Frank looked at Beryl questioningly.

'That will be his brother,' she said in a whisper, keeping an eye on the door and the ceiling above, as if someone might be listening or watching. 'He's bedridden, some kind of infantile paralysis, so people say. The Captain has looked after him ever since his mother died.'

There were sounds overhead; the opening of a window, the moving of a chair on lino and carpet. Then came the first bars of melody, vaguely familiar to Frank. The music strengthened and swelled into a drawling and powerful theme, strangely at odds with the smooth countryside around them.

The dog stirred to the music, grumbled a little under its breath and blinked at them with its old rheumy eyes. They looked round the study; it seemed much lived in, with burns on the hearthrug and dog's hairs on the furniture. It had a private and masculine air about it which did not entirely derive from the Alken sporting prints on the walls, or the close fragrance of tobacco, or even from the heavy, leather-bound classics that were ranked stolidly behind glass. To Frank, with the name of the tune evading him, the books had the static quality of goods in a shop window destined never to be bought.

Hearing their host's step on the stairs he whispered urgently to Beryl, 'But if his brother's ill, we can't possibly – '

She made a small, furious signal to him and turned to the dog, trying to cover her discomfiture by patting it and murmuring a meaningless phrase or two. But it seemed to know she was merely using it for some purpose of her own, and turned its old tousled head away, twitching a curly ear over one eye while tremors of indignation ran down to the blunt tail.

'I'm afraid Roger is too old and deaf to attend to people he doesn't know,' said the Captain, entering the room. He looked a little distracted as the music from the room above obtruded its melancholy over the whole house. 'Sorry to have left you.'

'I know what it is,' said Frank, with sudden excitement. 'It's *Pavane for a dead Infanta*.' It delighted him to recognise it, having been so long away from music. You couldn't count the stuff you got by turning a knob; it was a lot different from selecting your own record, dusting it off on your sleeve and laying it on the turntable, then poising the needle above the whirling black disc. Black magic, really. It had always given him a thrill.

'Damned depressing thing, anyway,' said the Captain with bitter emphasis, 'my brother's favourite. You'd think – ' but he dismissed whatever had come into his mind and was silent.

'How is he?' asked Beryl, 'I hope – '

'He has his ups and downs, and today he's not so well. I may get the doctor to take a look at him later on.' They both sensed the unrest behind the Captain's words, and Beryl, on whom illness acted as a stimulant, and whose concern made her almost beautiful, said, 'He's lucky to have such a good brother to take care of him,' and smiled.

'Lucky? He's not had a day's good luck for years. Not since our mother died, anyway. They were very attached.' He spoke stiffly, obviously not wanting to uncover any of the family grief. Then, shooting them a quick, impersonal look, he went on formally, 'Did you want to see me about anything, by the way?'

He looked at them quite kindly, but an uneasy movement of his hands showed that he wanted to break up this unsatisfactory tea party.

Frank rose immediately, speaking with haste, 'We won't keep you any longer, sir, but up on that hill I – we had the idea of calling on you. I thought maybe you might own some land, and we could buy half an acre or so, and build a little house . . .'

He felt Beryl's incredulous eyes on him, and knew she was reddening at his betrayal. The idea had just occurred to him, and now it seemed he had always had it. A little land, a house to build. Something salvaged after the shipwreck of the years. Something incredibly beautiful and lucky – a touchstone almost, after years when one's only possessions were a brief loincloth, two rice sacks sewn together, and the tattered remnants of a mosquito net. The idea excited him, his eyes shone.

'No,' said his wife strongly, moving her hands nervously on her lap. 'No, I'm sure we couldn't afford to buy land today, even with your gratuity, Frank. Then there's the cost of building . . .'

'I expect you both felt a little angry at the thought of this house standing half empty?' The Captain, who had been glancing from one to the other, spoke close on Beryl's words. 'I could see that something of the sort brought you both here. I was watching you come up the drive.'

They looked instinctively out of the window and there lay the curve of drive, the gate slightly ajar as they had left it, the lane beyond. They both looked and felt exposed. Nothing is so exposing as an action unknowingly overlooked. Worse was the feeling that they were no longer in the challenging position, it had passed to their host. As if realising this, he reached up to the mantelpiece for a pipe. He shook out the charred tobacco into an ashtray shaped like a horseshoe, which was mounted on a small leather saddle from which dangled two silver stirrups. It hung over the arm of his chair. From a bent tin he refilled the pipe carefully, shielding it as if from a stiff wind, and the intimacy of this lonely action made Frank come alive to their homelessness. The man before him might be lonely, but he had a home around him, the stability of rooms to walk into, doors to open and shut, lengths of corridors before him. He went restlessly to the window.

There was a long silence, then the Captain said, 'I can't help you, I'm afraid.' His tone was formal. 'I know everyone is crying out for houses and being fobbed off with electrically heated coffins instead. Your generation is different from mine. Do you know my great grandfather built a good deal of this house himself? He planned it not for years but for centuries. The family have added since; they acquired land and lost it. I sold the last bit of timber a few years ago. So you see, I've no land to speak of. True, I own a cottage or two, but my tenants pass them on to their sons and daughters. The country people are not afraid of a little discomfort – they think it more important to sink their roots deep – '

'Do you think we don't then?' Beryl interrupted, flushed with anger. 'Now let me tell you a few things. We were married only three months before Frank was sent out East. We were living in a furnished room, trying to get our things together gradually. I think he'd been abroad, yes, seven weeks, when we lost even that one room. Lost everything, in fact. Oh, I'm not trying to make a tragedy of it, it happened to too many people. What we want now is a chance to build something up again.' At that, she rose. She didn't look at the Captain. 'Let's go, Frank.'

She turned towards the door with a dignity Frank had never seen in her before. For a moment he saw in her eyes and attitude the enduring and undefeated purpose and care that women carry with them in adversity. He was comforted and made a little ashamed of his previous impatience with her.

'Yes,' he said, moving towards her, 'she's right. And although it's unworthy of me to say so, *I'd* like a little peace, too. I'm tired of fighting.'

The Captain's voice reached out to them harshly. 'You never stop fighting if you're a man. It's as much a part of life as breathing. Look around you and you'll see that the unhappiest men are those who have stopped fighting. They're full of apathy. You've got to struggle for what you want.'

'We want a house,' said Beryl bitterly. She was on the verge of tears and abruptly turned and went through the door into the hall. It seemed as if she could not bear the sound of the Captain's voice any longer. Upstairs, someone called faintly. She quickened her step to the front door, twisted it open with relief and stepped out on to the porch. Behind her the two men were shaking hands. Their eyes met as if discovering some essential, puzzling companionship that had come too late. Frank looked with regret into the dark hallway, feeling a chill of disappointment at the thought that they would in all probability never set foot there again.

Beryl turned a composed social face to the Captain, shook

hands briefly, thanked him for their tea like a well-behaved child. Then the door was shut and they walked down the drive together, soberly. In the lane the tall bank topped by the patchy white frills of blackthorn cut off the last dazzling rays of the evening sun. It was cold. But this time, as his wife hurried him along, with little remarks about the chilly air not being good for him, he did not draw away in resentment. Instead, he quickened his pace to please her, smiling to himself at the odd thoughts that crossed his mind – that, although irritating, there were worse things to be borne than a woman's solicitude.

'Poor old man,' said Beryl suddenly, 'I suppose we couldn't expect him to understand.'

* * *

Captain Banks went upstairs slowly. He was sure his brother would only want the gramophone wound again, that confounded record put on. Now something cheerful would be more to the point, something like – what *was* the tune? *Forty-seven Ginger-headed Sailors*, that was jolly and easy to hum. Pity the record was broken. Never mind, he could talk over the visit with his brother, tell him all about those two – he would like that. Young people today had no solid ground under their feet, they were to be pitied. The Captain shuddered at the vision of the dangerous twentieth century stretching before them, the mad pass to which science had brought the world.

As he opened the bedroom door he noticed that his spaniel had followed him up, and now ran quickly ahead of him. Wondering at the dog's haste, he entered a little heavily; the constant journeys up and down stairs were tiring.

His brother was sitting in a sideways position, resting on his elbow; his other hand was on the turntable of the gramophone, but his head had sunk down. In sudden anxiety the Captain ran to the bed, pushing the bed-table away and calling his name. He laid him down on the crumpled pillows, looking into his face, feeling for his pulse. Almost without thinking he turned to the gramophone, wound it up with the speed of panic and started off the record once more.

As the first notes came drawling out in a melancholy procession he felt a twinge of liking for the music. It certainly had grandeur – a black Spanish kind. His brother's face seemed to alter, the lines on it relaxed and he might have been a boy of thirteen to whom suffering was a new thing. He tried to nod in approval, smiled and said, 'That's it. That's what I called you for. Can't understand why you don't – like – it.' His voice faded on the last words.

The Captain knelt by the bed, at a loss. What could he feel, expecting this for so long? He made himself look into the dying man's face. 'Jo,' he said, 'Johnnie boy.' But John's face looked cold; the eyes were open. He waited for them to blink, turn, move. They did nothing. Then Roger scrabbled his old paws on to the bed, sniffed and dropped to the floor with a low mewing grunt. I always thought dogs howled, thought the Captain with a detached interest. Perhaps Roger's too old. Good thing. 'A mercy mother was not here to see it,' he went on, talking to himself, 'a long time and pain all the way, Johnnie boy.' Then he saw that Roger was up on his hind legs again, smelling John's face curiously, whimpering like a scolded child. And all at once he felt ridiculous on his knees. He rose, made to cover the face of the man on the bed, changed his mind. Better to let the evening sun fall on him as it sank for the last time. Mechanically he flicked off the record, and called the dog from the room.

Going heavily down the stairs, he pondered on the suns he had seen, swallowed up by the vivid seas, falling behind hills, dissolving in cloud. Never the last one for him, though. And looking out of the small window at the bend of the stairs, he thought, *but why not?* The valley had no more secrets from him; the seasons changed it only as clothes changed a woman. *Why not?* If I wanted, this could be the last sunset for me. No one left to grieve. He sighed, the weight of his intention penetrating his whole being; then continued down the stairs.

Arriving back in his own little room, he sensed an unfamiliar stir in the atmosphere, saw three cups on the table. He frowned, then suddenly remembered. Those two. Now what had he been about to do when they disturbed him? His eye fell on his gun in the corner. Ah, supper for Monsoon. Poor old feller'd be hungry, waking up and ruffling his wings, looking like a harassed professor. Smiling a little he went towards the gun, but something made him withdraw his hand. Not yet, not yet. Let's think first. After all, it was not quite dark, he could still bring down a small bird. The curlews were still crying, whirling in circles over the darkening fields like dancers on an invisible floor, with their light beautiful rhythms. He remembered a dancer he had seen in one of the Spanish ports. Warm, dark, smelling unpleasant when she circled near. The curlews were different, were black and white, elegant; cold and austere as this English spring. Sitting on the couch, his hand on Roger's head, the Captain repeated the word aloud, 'Curlew, curlew,' until all meaning was lost, all cohesion.

Feeling the need for some action, for the house was a dark weight in his head and on his heart, he started to walk through the rooms on the ground level. First the dining room, long and dark, heavy with oil paintings, massive with mahogany. He soon came out, wanting no reminders of the dinners of the past. At the beginning of his retirement he had tried to keep up the large dinner parties his mother had delighted in. But with no woman as hostess, calmly directing the flow of food and talk, he soon gave up. Now, walking into the drawing room, he preferred to think of John and himself as boys, coming down to dessert as a treat; of himself nearly swallowing a peach stone, his eyes were so dazzled by the largeness and bareness of a bosom across the table, just on a level with his eyes.

The drawing room, once white and gilt, now no colour – unless neglect has a colour of its own; a greyness of mould, of spiders' spinning, of the secret drifting dust – was high-ceilinged and gave on to the garden. It had many delicate chairs with stiff brocade cushions. The Captain threaded his way through the thin legs of the chairs and occasional tables, going straight towards a bureau placed by the French windows. He noticed with irritation that a sprig, a tendril of wisteria was twining through the hinge. 'Johnson's wife would soon clear that away,' he caught himself saying in the soundless mutter he unconsciously assumed when alone. It wasn't until a moment afterwards, when he had found what he was looking for, that he realised what he had said. He sat, with his hand suspended over an open drawer, asking himself *why?*

Impatiently he took up the book, then put it down again on the bureau top. His eye was caught by the garden outside. The shadows fascinated him. Usually he went through the stone kitchen and scullery to the garden but now he did not feel inclined to make the circuit. He wanted to walk out into the paved forecourt, go through the yew walk into the overgrown rose garden as if it were no new thing. The doors were stiff, they took him longer to open than the walk through the kitchen, but he did not mind. He shivered a little as he stepped through the doors, for the bulk of the house threw a shadow across this part of the garden. He noted with mild astonishment that the stones were pushed up unevenly, and bending down he realised that the tough roots of the wisteria were to blame. That and the spreading ferns and weeds.

'Gone to the dogs,' he said aloud. Then he straightened his shoulders and called to Roger, finding comfort in the stocky, curly body of the dog as it sniffed about in this unusual territory. 'How the time goes, like water through the hand.' How long ago since he had come home for good? Ten, fifteen years? His mother in the garden, stooping over the roses at a garden party. What would she say to this neglect? Something had to go, with two bachelors keeping house; and they hadn't done so badly, after all. His eye was startled by a whole flower-bed full of the first leaves of the treacherous ground-elder, and he bent to pull some up. His hand encountered an underground network of the pale, creeping roots, and disgusted, he kicked the patch, straightened and walked on.

The great yew hedge was unchanged, and he leaned his full weight against it, solid as a wall. From here he could look back on the house, really *see* it with all its possibilities. The sky flaming above it, the garden and creepers green below it. Wasn't that what they wanted, those two? A house, something to build? Fancy, calling when Jo was upstairs, dying alone . . . he had never known who had called. The Captain had never had a chance to talk them over with him. The thought obscurely worried him.

He beat at the solid hedge behind him. Never mind, Jo had missed so much already, he wouldn't regret not hearing about two strangers calling on the offchance for a house. A vision of the parties, picnics, excursions of all kinds Jo had missed came unbearably to his mind. Mother had always stayed with him, reading to him, talking – the Captain wondered what they had found to talk about – playing the piano and later the gramophone (he remembered the dusty mounds of records in Jo's bedroom). Ay, Jo must've missed her terribly when she died. He himself had been poor comfort in those slow nights of pain. He could never keep awake, sitting up beside him. He would nod off, wake up to find Jo still propped up, his eyes still open, smiling a little at his brother flopping over the pillows – he'd often tuck the eiderdown round him . . .

Roger was running round, pushing his nose into the unaccustomed hedges and overgrown flower-beds. Sometimes he pricked himself on a hidden rose thorn and retreated quickly. The Captain called him and fondled his ears, but could not make himself move from the hedge. Turning round about, he could take in the whole garden – tennis court, lawns, rockeries.

'It wouldn't take much more than hard work to restore this, old boy,' he said, 'and for anyone who wanted to build something up . . .' he checked himself abruptly. Hadn't he said that before? The tired face of the young man before his eyes, an ordinary face with a scar. Saw his wife, sturdy, warm-blooded. How unlike his own mother! She had been cool and unhurried. The young man's wife reminded him of the women he had taken in his strange ports of call during his long sailing life. There had been a kind of controlled desperation about them; women of the earth he suddenly saw they were, uprooted, with the rhythm of life destroyed for them. *Uprooted*, that was a significant word for the times. He saw the man's wife now as the symbol of a million homeless women, each one striving with the determination of the first woman to make a secure, warm place for her man, her child.

'She wants a house,' he said aloud in a puzzled voice, 'well now, what *is* a house?' His laugh went through the silent evening. Above his head something squeaked in flight, not a bird. The curlew had stopped its intricate pattern making. There was the challenge of an owl from a nearby tree; far away a dog was barking, a tireless, nightlong bark. But still the Captain did not move, although Roger was uneasy, peering round the pedestal of a chipped Pan with his pipes. 'Beginning of everything, that's certain. First thing animals do is to find a hole, line it with something soft, dig deeper to make it safe. Birds the same. But to us, as so-called civilised human beings? Can be a ship, can be a coffin.' He started along the path, his hand sweeping the close texture of the hedge, it was solid, gave him assurance. 'I've sailed many seas over. Know the smell of it, often cursed the spray putting out my pipe. I've often thought about it, standing in these hills. Often thought how like a calm sea were all these meadows, how like petrified storm billows the hills. Even this house, smoking away in a hollow, could be a ship I'd sailed with my impossible hopes, sailed into harbour.' He spoke jerkily, in the tone of a man accustomed to being alone with his thoughts; now he was in a sea dream, a man moving along a yew hedge with his forehead shining in the dusk and the dew coming on to his fingers from the leaves. 'This harbour for me, then, and what have I found here? Illness, decay, emptiness.' He called sharply to the dog, now out of sight, maybe scenting the intrusion of a rabbit, and started rapidly back across the garden. Despite his crowding thoughts and one intention the idea of Monsoon waking to hunger in the quiet attic worried him.

He was almost in the drawing room when he heard a soft growling from the spaniel. Turning, he saw him coming towards the house, tail wagging, carrying something in his mouth. It was a small field mouse. The tiny thing was dead, and the Captain looked as surprised as did the dog. 'That was luck and nothing else,' he said laughing, patting the dog's head and gently taking the little body. 'You've solved Monsoon's problem, anyway.'

Going through the doorway, he caught sight of the book he had been looking for, then forgotten. He took it up and went with it to his study. There he lighted a candle and sat on the couch, the dead mouse on the table before him, the windows uncurtained. It was an album; photographs and long pages of his mother's sloping handwriting. She had described every incident of their childhood, and illustrated the story by drawings and sepia photographs. There was even a piece of silk pinned above an account of one Christmas party. 'Dear little Bertie looked so pretty in his new silk blouse: I had Miss Pargeter in to make it for him, with matching velveteen trousers.'

He turned the pages with absorbed interest, seeing the captured incidents of a confident past as solid memories, the real life. He noticed the entries relating to himself grew less when he went to boarding school.

The gun was still leaning in the corner.

Then he saw that all his letters had been pinned in, letters from school, from the training ship, from ports all over the world. 'Bertie writes such interesting letters. I wonder what will become of him? Some of the things he says are Clever . . . I wonder if he will become a Great Sailor?'

Again, 'John derives great Comfort from his Brother's letters. Last night I sat up with him and read over the last six or seven. He does not seem to resent the lack of excitement in his own life. I hope Bertie will take Care in these foreign ports.'

There it is, just by my hand.

He shut the book. Then with a gentler hand, turned to

the title page, 'This Book is for those who come after us, that they shall know what Manner of People we were.' She had ornamented this sentence with scrolls as stiff as the words themselves. Perhaps she had written and designed the florals with that indrawn, self-conscious look he had sometimes surprised on her face. He turned slowly to the last entry. 'Bertie is expected home tomorrow. His last trip is over. He has done well and deserves his retirement. From the bottom of my heart I thank the good Lord for his preservation through many Perils.'

His eye fell on the mouse and he took it up and left the room almost at a run. There were many things to be done. Up in the attics he whistled once, and there was a flurry of wings. Monsoon sat expectantly on a beam. The Captain dangled the mouse by the tail and the owl, in a swift sweep, caught it up in his beak. His soft headfeathers brushed the Captain's cheek. Before he left the attic he tore down the wire netting from the window. 'Off you go,' he said.

Downstairs, he pulled out a Will form, sat down at his desk with pen and ink and fulfilled the first part of his intention. 'I hereby bequeath . . . my home, land and all household effects to Frank Johnson and his wife, Beryl Johnson. Also five hundred pounds to enable them to carry out necessary repairs to the house and garden.' Then followed the appointment of executors; he thought a moment over that and then put down the name of his bankers. He added a few personal bequests and a legacy or two to old friends, then blotted the will, put it in a long envelope and calling Roger once more, went from the house.

He hummed a little going up the lane, and after walking about a quarter of a mile, turned in at a cottage. Old George Evans and his wife were at their bread and cheese and onion supper and were surprised to see him. Although they were his tenants, he rarely called on them. Rising from his chair as his wife showed the Captain in, his hand went to the teapot. 'Cup o' tea, Captain?'

'Yes please, George,' said the Captain and sat down.

After a desultory conversation he pulled out the Will and said, 'Will you witness this, you and Mrs. Evans?'

The old couple looked a little startled.

'What? put my name to it, Captain?' said the old man. 'Have we any ink, Mary?'

His wife found a half-bottle on the window sill and a pen with a shaky nib. Rubbing her hands on her apron, she signed where the Captain indicated, shaking her head as if to put away the thoughts the sight of this legal paper brought her. Then her husband signed, and Captain Banks stood up.

He pulled out a couple of notes, put them on the table, and hesitating, said, 'I'm much obliged to you, and now there's one more thing. May I leave Roger here with you? He knows you.'

George frowned in bewilderment, bent down to pat the dog. 'Are you going away for long, Captain?' he asked.

But Captain Banks was bending over the dog, telling him to stay there. 'Good chap,' he said, 'good chap.' He did not seem to hear the old man's question.

At the door he looked round the room, at Roger; and

141

again he said, 'I'm very much obliged. God bless you both. Good night.'

Old George looked out into the darkness, and smelt the sharp rain on the wind. Then he went in and closed the door.

The Captain, walking in the first fine rain of the night, had a jumble of cool thoughts in his head. 'An extraordinary day,' he said, half turning to address the dog who was no longer there, 'one might almost say momentous.'

The gun is leaning in the corner and the candle will be burnt out.

THE PRISONER

It was a frosty morning when the German prisoners first
came to dig drainage ditches in the fields that lay beyond
Miss Everton's garden walls. She was out with her dog in the
chill air by the beech trees when two large lorries roared
up past her across the grass and she had a glimpse of alien
faces, of packed cardboard figures, cold and raw-looking. The
rest of the valley was quiet, as if sheltered beneath a glass bell
of cold and solitude. The hills stretched far beyond the fields
and farms, the little trees on their sides standing straight and
close, like stitches on an old tapestry.

The trees that outlined the remains of a carriage drive
across the fields to the lane beyond still kept their leaves,
however, and each morning Miss Everton came to look at
them. They seemed to her an echo of the past long and
temperate summer, but somehow odd, like fruits out of
season. Here the trees were later shedding their leaves, but
by November the gales had usually stripped them bare; it
was nearly November now. Only the tough marigolds in the
garden still went on producing their frostbitten suns; in the
house a patch of brightness across a room, through a closed
window, gave back summer's ghost.

143

The sun was coming up now, a long way off in the clear blue of the sky. But it warmed Miss Everton's hands, cold and clenched on the sticks she had gathered so that she could look away from the men as they jumped from the backs of the lorries. For some time they had been calling to each other in mirthless foreign voices, groaning with stiffness and cold, beating their hands together with a sound that carried in the petrified air.

A rustle disturbed her, made her straighten up. It was a sound she knew, furtive as fox or rabbit creeping through the starched grass: the leaves had begun to fall. They fell from ash and rowan, from lime and sycamore, they fell straight down through the still air, but with no haste. It was as if each leaf – green or yellow, brown or spotted grey – paused before relinquishing its hold, and this pause gave Miss Everton the impression that the pale sun had been a signal, was in fact their puppet master. Fascinated, she watched their regulated ballet, their unregretful, unhurried surrender. The patter increased, the tempo seemed to quicken, the air was full of falling leaves.

'Excuse me, could we get any water from the cottage? Are you the owner?'

At the sound of a human voice Miss Everton turned her head unwillingly. A young man stood by her side, also staring at the trees. He watched one or two leaves drop twirling from the sycamore, hesitating before they settled on the chastened grass. 'It's all a matter of contraction and expansion, I suppose,' he went on. She noticed he wore leather leggings and was obviously in charge of the working party.

'Yes, it's my cottage. There's a tap in the garden you can use.' She purposely ignored his explanation, wanting him to go as quickly as possible. So few people called on her that when someone did it was intolerable. All the same, she could not help adding that she used the garden tap to water her flowers. She was proud of her water supply, achieved after much fuss, piped from the hill right into her house.

'I'd be grateful if we could use it to water some less attractive objects,' said the young man, jerking his head towards the prisoners, who now stood with picks and shovels in the middle of the field. 'Still, they're better than Italians any day. All song and no work, those 'tallies. Now I wouldn't call the Jerries exactly cheerful, but – '

'I'll show you where the tap is,' Miss Everton said, and led the way to the cottage. The young man shrugged, beating his legs with a switch. He was only trying to be friendly, on a job like this a friendly woman, even if she was middle-aged, could make a lot of difference. But Miss Everton was not feeling friendly. She did not like the young man's voice, nor the things he said. It was useless to tell herself that he was young, and only the young could ally with their innocence a certain cynicism, a certain brash cruelty that supported them, seeing as they did the world falling in pieces around them. Also, she told herself, he had probably seen the Germans under very different circumstances, and to have them (or a cross-section of them) under his command was an uncomfortable experience. The thrill for him had undoubtedly been in the chase, not the capture. As he tested the tap, and talked on with that touch of a ringmaster's arrogance, Miss Everton began to fathom his feelings towards the prisoners; it was a sort of distorted pity, which made him despise both them and himself.

Later that morning, when the day had settled down to its accustomed autumnal chill, alleviated by thin sunshine, she heard the water hum and sing through the pipes. Startled, for she had become absorbed in her housework, she peered out of an upstairs window and saw two of the prisoners drawing water. She did not go downstairs, but stayed watching them as they straightened up and went out of the gate, pulling it shut after them. She noticed that the taller of the two looked searchingly at the cottage before following his companion across the field. The thought occurred to her that even if they tried to escape, they could not get very far, the round yellow patches on their uniforms stood out as clearly as targets.

When they had disappeared she prepared her lunch, but she was restless. How long were they going to be there? How many times a day would her gate click open and the pipes hum and sing as the prisoners drew water? It was more than disturbing, she told herself, they were too near altogether, only a field away. She knew that the thought of them working in the cold would hang like a shadow over her own work – doubtless she would hear whistles marking their rest periods; twice a day the lorries would roar past.

Never mind, Miss Everton told herself firmly, tomorrow I shall speak to them. All the afternoon she rehearsed a few German phrases, wanting to hand them out, like comforts, to the silent men. After all, they were not of her generation, she had known an older Germany; lustier, lusher, more prosperous: gayer. As a girl she and her brother Humphrey

146

had gone off on trips together – he had studied at Bonn and she had picked up a good deal of slangy, everyday talk, although she had never been able to carry on much of a discussion in the language. But then she had never had much occasion to argue – the young men she met did not argue with women. They merely danced with them, walked with them, made sentimental love to them. How did these poor fellows manage? she wondered suddenly. She found herself half turning to ask Humphrey about it, and his loss came once more as a bitter pain. She missed more than anything, now she was nearing fifty, not having anyone to whom she could say, 'Do you remember?' For at this moment she was remembering acrid black coffee at Aachen at one o'clock in the morning, drunk from cardboard cups. Shutting her eyes, she recalled exactly the chill of the platform as the train halted for ten minutes or so before pulling over the border. How cold she had been! That, and the crumpled, sour feeling of travelling all night, had remained as one of her most vivid recollections of the holiday. She scarcely remembered now the rocky islands of the Rhine, rising out of a dawn that would have seemed more real on the stage of Covent Garden, with barbaric and hysterical music uniting the boxes to the gallery.

At four o'clock, settled down over her books and type-writer, Miss Everton heard the pipes sing once more. She did not move. Her lips rehearsed a greeting, but she could not bring herself to go to them – what if they looked at her dumbly, with dislike or amusement? Still she sat on, knowing that soon they would be gone for the day and the opportunity of showing them that someone in this cold northern corner of

England had known the dark-green Harz mountains and the gentle Bavarian country, would be lost. Sure enough, half an hour later, she heard a thin whistle and soon after the lorries churned past. She was grateful for the garden wall and the thick trees around the cottage – terrible if the men could gaze in the window and see her sitting there, lonely over her tea.

Leaving the teapot warming by the fire, Miss Everton suddenly rose up, called Tag, and together they went across the tightening ground in the failing light. She stopped by the big tree in the middle of the field. The fire was still smouldering. On either side a sharpened stake stood erect, the top shaped like a catapult. Across this the men obviously laid another stick and hung their tins from it over the flames. Miss Everton smiled. That was clever, it really was! Somehow it made the whole thing seem like a game, played with the same absorption as Boy Scouts on a camping holiday. It reminded her of the gipsies of two summers ago; she had often watched the caravans, floating like lighted boats on the rising ground mist of early September.

The blackened tins swung from the tree above her making dry sounds in the slight wind. A pile of neatly cut logs and twigs waited for the next day: picks and other tools were stacked round the tree. Across the fields stretched a line of stakes; they must have spent the day measuring out the lines of ditches to be dug. Miss Everton shivered. Calling Tag, she returned home.

The evenings had once been her dread. Together, as they had been for so many years, she and Humphrey had defeated the weariness and claustrophobia forced on them by the grey

lowering skies or close darkness of winter, by reading aloud
to each other. They had chosen passages to fit the mood of
the elements. On stormy nights Humphrey would read
about the old gossips at the bar of the *Maypole* and of poor
Barnaby Rudge, who had in him the sweetness of some of
Shakespeare's fools. Summer evenings called for something
more serene, prose that pleased the mind, so they chose
Conrad's *Typhoon* (for Humphrey longed for the sea and the
tropics) or Lamb's lucid dissertations. This last choice was
Miss Everton's; she longed to reach back through the years
and comfort Lamb, seeing in his devoted life something akin
to her own and her brother's.

When Humphrey died – in the third year of the war, from
pneumonia contracted by crawling through wet bracken on a
useless Home Guard foray – she had not known what to do.
Her sense of loneliness was so complete, so terrible, that all
sense of the division between night and day went from her.
Her mind and body knew only coldness; she was consumed by
the fear of going mad. She was one of those people to whom
the Bible was a habit and not a consolation, and she lacked
the pure courage to follow philosophical thought; that way
was too bare, too cold. If she had ever had a really full life – if
she had ever been physically and mentally fulfilled, then the
courage might have come to her. As it was, having given up
the idea of marriage to be with Humphrey, and having only
one or two glances and caresses to hold in her mind as
evidence of that dangerous emotion, love, she watched them
go shoddy with years of conjuring up, as letters become thin
with too much handling.

She found her comfort in the village people. Living as they did with the churchyard in the centre of the village, with birth and death as inevitable as the spring and the fall of the year, they had a melancholy and yet unquestioning acceptance. This attitude at last seeped into Mary Everton's plunging mind and steadied her: she felt, after many months, a deeper sense of life itself. The next thing was to accustom herself to a new routine, for it was the small daily setting forth of one cup instead of two, of one bed to make, a smaller batch of weekend cakes, that troubled her.

But gradually she found another interest, one that was closely connected with Humphrey. She had always lent books to one or two of her friends, and had taken pleasure in suiting the book to the person. Now she went further; she started a small library in the village. With the co-operation of the Women's Institute she enrolled subscribers and went round buying books cheaply and begging volumes from friends' libraries. Slyly she introduced the village women to authors they had not read since leaving school. She widened her own reading and passed on her preferences to the others. She was adviser and secretary as well as librarian and treasurer. The work filled her evenings and she began to feel content.

This was the rhythm the coming of the German prisoners interrupted. It threw her out of key, so that instead of checking the library lists after her light supper (she combined tea and supper, boiling or poaching an egg each evening), she sat down and thought about the men who had arrived that day. She sighed, and shifted in her little low chair – for she was not a tall woman and liked to stretch out her legs before the fire – and wondered if their advent would upset her. She wished they would go away.

* * *

The cold set in with a new moon. The air seemed to contract, and the Germans went about the fields with a hunched, defensive walk, as if their flesh prickled with cold under the thick, rough khaki. They blew into their hands and beat their arms, they drew breath cautiously, as if it pained them to gulp down the icy, knife-sharp air. They returned reluctantly to their digging after their brief rests by the fire. In the middle of this cold snap a small hut appeared. A lorry brought it one morning. It had two central wheels and the men propped it up on tree trunks to keep it steady.

Miss Everton, watching shamelessly through her bedroom window, saw that it had a chimney and a window and a decent door. She was pleased, thinking that the men could eat their dinner in the warm. She knew two of them by name, for a few days ago one of them had knocked softly on her kitchen window, asking for a cardboard box. She had been startled, disconcerted; it was a signal from the cold, a challenge from the outcast. They watched each other through the closed, frosted window in that moment's hesitation; a solidly built young man and a small, ordinary-looking woman with a face like a startled mouse. She had given him an old shoe box and he went away; someone called him from the field. Erich.

Miss Everton went downstairs and busied herself with her cooking. She was mashing potatoes when she heard that soft knock again. This time she went to the door, and opened it. It was the same young man, his face red with cold. He held out a paper bag, full of something.

'You want tea?' he asked.

'Please come in,' she said, to gain time. He stepped inside gingerly, hauling his cap from his head. Once the door was shut he stood awkwardly, like a horse led to a new stable, his great rubber boots thick with mud and ice. His mild blue eyes were fixed on the bright coal fire and the steaming saucepan of potatoes, his hands were tough and weathered as a ploughboy's.

'Tea,' he said again, offering her the bag. She looked puzzled, and in explanation he went on, 'The chaps want to ask if you will give coffee in exchange.' His English was careful, free of mistakes; he had obviously been going over the words in his head. It seemed odd to her that the prisoners should be referred to as chaps – it was too free and easy, too English.

'*Bitte setzen Sie hier,*' murmured Miss Everton, pushing a chair up to the fire. She poured a cup of tea, for she had just made herself one as was her mid-morning custom, and handed it to him. He looked up at her with slight pleasure, although he did not comment on her German. She went to the larder and took out a two-pound tin of coffee and laid it on the table. Surely it wasn't illegal? No, she told herself firmly, exchange was perfectly legal. Also, she was often short of tea: one person living alone suffered worst from rationing.

She began to ask him questions; about himself, about his family. He told her he came from Saxony, from a small farm; now he wanted to go back to look after his mother. He did not seem to fear the fact that he would be living in the Russian zone. But Russians filled her with dread, she saw them as half-human, adorned with stolen wristwatches.

'What do we Germans deserve, anyway?' said Erich, shrewdly seeing her reactions.

But Miss Everton could not believe in this kind of humility. It did not match her own experience. It was intensely embarrassing to hear such a thing said – unless, of course, it was meant as mordant humour, directed as much against her as against himself. This helpless air, this ghost of self-pity, annoyed her. She felt sure that no Englishman in the same situation would have allowed these sentiments to creep into his attitude. But then, she told herself quickly, the English would never have allowed themselves to be defeated.

Erich thoughtfully laid down his cup. 'Yes,' he said. 'Yes, you are kind. I find good people wherever I go. In Canada, in South Wales – all good people if you look for them . . . ' He seemed puzzled at the thought of there being so many good people about, and yet the world itself being so unsatisfactory. 'We drink tea plain at the barracks,' he said suddenly, 'but it is nice with sugar and milk.'

Miss Everton could not imagine anyone drinking tea like that. She had to query it. 'We save our sugar to cook with, and the milk is in tins,' he explained. 'We don't bring any to work in the fields.'

'But you have a nice warm hut to eat your dinner in,' said Miss Everton, trying to be cheerful, and feeling that a prisoner ought not to complain.

'Hut? Oh . . . ' He looked at her with his face closed up into what, on subtler features, would be wryness. 'That is for the overseer, and for the papers and the tea. That is not for us.'

There was a tap at the window and he swung round. 'That is Kurt. I go at once, they are asking for me.' He took up the coffee and ducked his head. '*Danke schoen*, tomorrow we talk again.' And he was gone.

After that Erich called in often. Sometimes they had biscuits with their mid-morning cup of tea. She asked about his family, and learnt that his father was dead, that he sent his mother parcels when he could, that on the whole he was disappointed with England, finding it dirty and unfriendly. Miss Everton grew attached to him, as one does to a tentative mongrel dog or a small child, and humoured him, giving him sweet things to eat – as if her gifts could somehow assuage the times in which he had been born. Although she scarcely admitted it to herself, these small offerings – some coffee, or a tinned pudding or stew for his mother – helped to smother a niggling, inexplicable feeling of shame. She noticed that he never asked any questions about herself, and at first thought it was because of the barrier his imprisonment raised between them. Then she began to see, as the weeks passed and his mind became more familiar to her, that although he might discuss the outside world with her, to him other people's lives were like glimpses from a slow-moving train. One passed small gardens; in one a woman was putting her baby out in a pram, in another a man bent over his onion bed, children ran in and out of doorways like silverfish on a hearth. These were brief glimpses only, they offered no clue to the constant stream of life flowing away from the train, gave nothing but a temporary warmth. Erich dared not be too interested, possessing as he did the bewildered, blunted mind of the uprooted peasant.

There was one question Miss Everton wanted to ask him, however, and one day she did. How had he been captured? He told her quite simply that he had been in a submarine which had surrendered. Encouraged and forced on by something urgent in her own nature, Miss Everton asked in a voice that grew thin with embarrassment – as if she were committing a social gaffe – whether it was true that U-boat captains surfaced after destroying an enemy ship and shot all survivors.

He sat playing with her broken potato peeler, then said simply, 'Men do terrible things in a war; I have thought a lot about it.'

'Did you, did your captain shoot our men?' demanded Miss Everton again, her body growing cold.

Erich roared with laughter, watching her as he did so. 'We never hit a ship,' he replied. 'I was only at sea for a year and we seemed to go sailing up and down the coast of South America.'

'But why?'

'We were getting sunk, and U-boats don't like that. We were given a go-slow order.' He laughed again, as if cajoling her, then stood up, slipping the peeler into his pocket. 'See, I take this away and mend it for you.'

* * *

As the days drew nearer to Christmas the sun began to shine frostily. Miss Everton often felt the need for a walk. But

155

the usual one she took across the fields out to the farm, there to have a chat and a cup of tea with Mrs. Jones, the farmer's wife, was now blocked by the line of extending and deepening ditches. Rolls of barbed wire lay at various points, ready to be put into position as soon as the stakes were up. Looking out from her bedroom window at the number of men digging, she felt her first active pang of resentment since the lorries had first roared up across the fields. She, in effect, was the prisoner; the sun glinted on the barbed wire, the heaps of thrown-up earth glittered frostily. The fields were no longer free; she was watched wherever she went outside the walls of her garden.

Erich had mended her potato peeler, and when he brought it back he had handed her a present as well. He had made her a pair of bedroom slippers out of an unravelled, dyed and plaited sack. He had put leather soles on, and large bobbles on each toe. Miss Everton was as much touched by the ugliness of his gift as by the patient and ingenious work that had gone into the making of it. When he showed her some bracelets he had made out of some sort of plastic material, she offered to try and sell them to one or two of the women she knew in the village. It would bring him in a little extra money for Christmas.

When he came to the cottage next it was with a request. He asked her if she had any maps of South Wales – his friends there had asked him to spend the holiday with them. They were small farmers and he had worked on their land for a while; he told her that they had been like parents to him. If the distance was within the hundred-mile limit he would be allowed to go. Miss Everton, feeling his excitement as a personal thing, searched upstairs for a map and brought it down.

They spread it out on the table, looking for Pembrokeshire. It was worn and frayed at the folds, but still legible. With a ruler they measured out distances.

'Yes,' said Miss Everton at last, touched by the sight of those large fingers going tenderly over the names of places where he had once been able to make friends, 'it looks to me as if you might just be able to go.'

'Ah.' Erich straightened up, his eyes almost sparkling. 'To go on a train alone, and live in a house with a fire for two whole days, sleep without twenty other men – that will be wonderful.'

As he left her he whistled a little folk tune down the path, his boots crunching in the light fall of frozen snow.

The next day he was back again.

'So,' he said, stamping snow off his boots. 'I cannot go. I ask at the railway station to make sure, and we go over it, the stationmaster and I. It is twenty miles too far. I must stay in camp.' His eyes had a cold, disappointed look in them. Miss Everton was sure that he was determined not to complain, not to make a fool of himself and his hopes and disappointment. For the first time she fully approved of him; he was keeping any self-pity firmly in control. She asked him what they did in camp at Christmas time, and he told her in a cold, formal voice that they saved up for a good dinner and might have a concert in the evening. At home there would be a little tree and the cradle with the Child in it – his little sister would make a rag doll – only this year there would be no sugar sweets for her to hang on the tree. He did not stay long with her. It seemed as if he identified her, too, with the authority that spoilt his Christmas, and the drumming consciousness that he was a prisoner made any easy talk impossible. He left the cottage without his usual cup of tea.

That evening, when she was alone, instead of working on the accounts – she had neglected the library lately – Mary Everton sat and thought about him. She was grateful for the mended peeler and the gift of shoes, although she knew that he had given them to her to even them up a little – so that he did not seem to be leaning on her charity all the time. She felt that he deserved something else of her; she knew that from purely humanitarian motives she ought to ask him to spend Christmas with her. But what would the village people say, how would Mrs. Jones feel about it? Mrs. Jones had already asked her to spend Christmas Day with them, and she had accepted. She clung to this fact as she debated the reasons for and against. But wasn't it her duty to make at least one other person happy when the opportunity arose? There was little enough she could do about the callousness of the world; she ought then, surely, to try and improve her small corner of it. But what when he had gone, swallowed up in the Russian Zone? She would have to continue to live among the villagers, who never forgot anyone's departure from their accepted code. No, she couldn't do it.

The next day she caught the early bus into the nearest market town. The shops were decorated; in the largest one a woman disguised as Father Christmas stood at the door and stamped her feet, occasionally lifting her cotton wool beard to carry on a conversation with a passing acquaintance. This shocked Miss Everton profoundly, thinking of the bitter disillusion such an action would have on any trusting child brought up to believe in Father Christmas. She carried on with her Christmas shopping, and spent, as always, much more than she had intended. She had lunch and went to the pictures in the afternoon. But even as she watched the screen, flickering into momentary life in black and white, she wondered what Erich would think if he had come to the window that morning and found her away. She clasped her parcels as if to excuse herself, for in one of them was an expensive warm scarf and a pair of gloves for him, jumpers for his mother and sister, and a small box fitted with sewing materials. She was giving him gifts, so why did she feel uncomfortable, unaccountably mean? Oh, she would be glad when they had all gone! The parked lorries, the overseer's hut, the barbed wire, the prisoners spread silently over the fields – all gone to some other part of the country. It wasn't fair, this intrusion.

The next day the first person she saw was the young overseer. As usual, he was rinsing out his mug at the tap. Miss Everton would associate the tap with him long after he was gone, she thought suddenly.

'Well,' he said, watching as she shook out her kitchen mat, 'we'll be off before Christmas after all. Leave you in peace then. Some of this lot will be home in the Fatherland in the New Year; things are speeding up. We leave here Christmas Eve.' He added grudgingly, 'They've done a good job.'

Miss Everton's cold hands dropped the mat, mechanically she slapped Tag as he tried to worry the strings of her apron. 'Christmas Eve,' she repeated slowly. 'Why, that's the day after tomorrow. So you've finished, then?'

He looked at her jauntily. 'That's right,' he said. Miss Everton went indoors. She took stock of her larder, then started to mix a cake. It was ready for the oven when Erich came for water with another man. He smiled and waved but did not come in. Perhaps he was keeping away because he could not bear her to talk to him in her usual friendly way and not ask him the one thing he wanted to hear. Tears came to her eyes as she put the cake in the oven.

The following morning she iced it, first putting a thick layer of almond paste on the top, made with soya flour and almond flavouring, which was the best she could do. She found she was talking aloud to herself. 'After all,' she said, smoothing the paste with a rolling pin, 'when our men were prisoners, the farmers' wives gave them basins full of mashed turnips to eat, like animals. Humphrey would agree, I'm sure. I can't do it – even for the sake of the holidays we had over there. When you're young you can be happy anywhere; it's stupid to feel so guilty, so heavy-hearted about it.' At least, she told herself, he should have his cake with a miniature Father Christmas on the top. And some mince pies. Anyway, what would she do with a man in the house all day? He would disturb her routine, and what would they find to talk about? The hours would hang too heavily. Dismissing the idea with an impatient shake of her head, she put the decorated cake into the larder.

The next day he came to see her for the last time.

'Today is Christmas Eve,' he said, and on his tongue the words were heavy with nostalgia, with an ancient tradition of goodwill and kindliness. 'I want to thank you for all you have done, it has meant a lot to me. I have to say goodbye now.' He hesitated, 'In a month or less I go back to Germany.'

'Do you really want to go back?' she asked. So this was their last meeting, her last link with the cold outer world which suffered and went hungry and were separated. 'Couldn't you –' She caught a look on his face as he glanced sharply at her. She finished lamely, 'couldn't you stay over here somehow?'

'How? My father dead, my mother growing old, with a farm to see to? She needs me with her.' After a pause he went on, with a trace of disbelief, 'Anyway, there may be some good Russians who will let me work on in peace. I am lucky with people. After all, we are all separate men and women, no? We each think with our own heads and feel with our own hearts, whatever salute our hands must give.' He put down his cup, for his hands were trembling. 'Miss Everton, do you believe in God?'

Miss Everton was taken by surprise, for he spoke under stress. The words that had come out in his halting but accurate English were only spurts of the ones that boiled in his mind. His whole being, as he sat there, was like a reined dynamo. She felt he wanted to stand up and smash something, cry out with anguish at his situation. It was the kind of despair, she felt, that the English were saved from, the despair that had always racked Europe and showed itself in the suicide pacts between the young men after the First World

War, in the novels of the nineteenth-century Russian writers. It was there in Erich's motionless figure, sitting in her kitchen. What answer could she give, what comfort was there to offer him? She was not a philosopher, nor a politician, nor a saint; she was a woman only, and a limited one.

She went to the larder.

'Of course I believe in God,' she said in a severe voice, as if surprised at the question. 'He works in an inscrutable way. He tests each of us to the limit of our endurance. Now here is a cake I have baked for you, and some mince pies.' Let these comfort him where I cannot, she thought, and displayed the cake for him to see before packing it into a box. Instantly his face lost the strained look and she realised that, like herself, he was not accustomed to thinking largely, and therefore small things – a cake or a kindness – could dismiss certain of his fears.

She left him there and hurried from the kitchen. In her sitting-room was an array of parcels, wrapped in coloured paper and tied with tinsel string, each labelled. She picked up two of them, and went back to Erich. He was regarding the cake with serious, melancholy eyes.

'I hope – I – *fröhliche Weinachten!*' she said in a rush, and tumbled the presents into his hands. It was obvious that he did not know what to say. He just clasped them to him and looked up at her. A tap at the window saved them from the embarrassment of thanks and protestations, and hurriedly Miss Everton began parcelling up the cake and the mince pies, telling him to share them with his friends if he wanted to, and to wish them all a happy Christmas from her.

At the door they said goodbye. Miss Everton held out her hand, but he had difficulty in clasping it because he was so laden. On impulse she stood on tiptoe and kissed him gently on the cheek. 'God bless you,' she said, and closed the door.

She stood and looked at it for a long time, then went quietly to her room and took down her hair before the mirror. She brushed it continuously while tears flowed down her cheeks; she could not stop them. It became a desolate rhythm, the strokes of the brush against her long soft hair and the tears chasing down her cheeks. Usually this ritual of hair-brushing soothed her when she felt her nerves tight and jangled, but it was a long time before it had that effect today. She could not push away the picture of Erich looking in at other people's Christmases through their lighted windows. At last, exhausted and cold, she lay on her bed, pulling the eiderdown over her, and stared out of the window. Tag was whining at the door, doubtless the fire would be low; she dropped into an unhappy day sleep.

She didn't know at first what had awakened her. Here was her room, the rumpled bedclothes that did not belong to the neutral light of a winter afternoon. Then she gradually realised what she was listening to – the harsh, growing throb of engines preparing to move off. She knew this sound so well that she did not really need to stumble to the window to watch the lorries moving off for the last time. The little hut bowled along behind on its two wheels.

She felt a panicky desire to shout after them. Although she knew that within a month or two the men inside would be facing conditions that she, and everyone else in this country, would find intolerable, it seemed to her that they were free, and once again she the imprisoned one.

She went downstairs, thinking to make herself a cup of tea, but the heavy silence and the sullen fire defeated her. She called Tag, reproachfully half asleep on the mat, nose down to his paws, and together they left the cottage. A few minutes later she was contemplating the blackened tins hanging from the large beech tree, the still warm ashes of the fire, and the deep raw ruts the wheels had torn in the frozen earth. Not one of them, she thought, with a slight, inexplicable pang, had had the heart to cut his initials into the tree. Maybe that sort of gesture sprang from happiness, she told herself, remembering linked hearts in the woods; from a desire to remember and be remembered. As it was, all marks of them would soon be gone; the ashes scattered, the ruts grown over with bright spring grass, the tins and few cut sticks seized by questing children. If she excepted the ditches, with the glinting barbed wire and the straight, deep sides, along which water already tinkled, things would soon be just as if they had never come. And, after all, ditches could be dug by anybody, anybody at all.

She went on telling herself this until she was indoors again, raking up the fire, putting on a kettle. It was not until she sat down, with her cup of tea beside her, that she suddenly put her head in her hands. For she knew that nothing would ever be the same again.

AFTERWORD

□□□□□□□

A fitting start to this memoir might be Paul Scott's poem, found in my journal for 1943.

The brief days of Youth
And its forgotten past,
cannot be commanded to appear.
We hope they will at last
– some other time – some other year.

Not a marvellous poem. But Paul was young when he wrote it, as we all were. When I copied it down, with no comment, inbetween the daily entries of that first summer at our cottage in North Wales, I had no idea how long it would take for that 'some other time' to arrive.

My writing life began, I suppose, in the hot, growly summer of 1939. At the age of nineteen I had done a bunk from the nice safe job chosen for me at the Bank of England and, without telling my family, had found a niche writing captions for a photographic News Agency. 'Spring Bounds into Hyde Park' (Ducks, daffodils and dogs), 'A Splashing Good Time' (Bathers fronting waves breaking over rocks on some forgotten shore).

Then, one lunch time, to escape a sharp summer storm, I walked into a bookshop in Victoria Street. The tall young man behind the counter was arranging piles of large red books: *Household Management*. Then he wrote out a label in a beautiful hand: 'All going at One Shilling each.' I wandered round the shelves, shaking out my wet hair.

I ordered a book, although he must have known I was not a serious customer. You can always tell, he said later. We got into an earnest conversation: about the coming war, about pacificism, about books. There was between us an instant recognition, as if we had been a long time waiting for this meeting. The world took a sidestep away.

Years later, on a wedding anniversary, a parcel was left on the breakfast table. A Penguin Science Fiction reprint of Olaf Stapledon's *Last and First Men*. On the flyleaf was written: 'Ordered from Victory Bookshop August 1939 – delivered by hand April 1964. Glad to be of service, madam.'

Both of us had been brought up in safe London suburbs, in safe London families, although Reginald had left home some years before. Now, at the outbreak of war, I welcomed the challenge of living with him in the heart of things and at the edge of danger. A Bayswater bed-sit could be rented for 17/6 a week if you didn't mind making do with a curtained-off alcove with a sink, a tap and a gas ring. A 1/- in the slot gas fire, a reasonably comfortable clean bed, a wardrobe, two chairs, a table, shelves and a somewhat threadbare carpet or rug.

What more do you need when life is so rich?

Reginald would never take a place until he had tried out his portable gramophone in the empty wardrobe. He would put on – say – 'The Swan of Tuonela' and carefully manipulate the door. If the acoustics were right, we would take the room. At night we walked through Bayswater and Notting Hill Gate before the raids began; round Ladbroke Grove where a racecourse had once been. The blacked-out cliffs of tall rooming houses fronting the secret squares, the huge reddish moon that hung low over the empty streets, seemed like props on a deserted stage waiting for the action to begin. No one has caught the atmosphere of those moonlit nights better than Elizabeth Bowen in her story 'Mysterious Kôr'.

Reginald had published his first novel with Michael Joseph, which coincided with the Munich crisis and suffered accordingly despite good reviews. He had also had short stories in a number of magazines. Now his ambition was to found a literary magazine that would, in his own words, 'widen the opportunity for young writers of talent and bring in a cross-section of society.' He was convinced that writers had a major part to play in the war. 'Do we ever really know,' he asked in one of his provocative editorials, 'the precise nature of what we have gone through until our writers recreate it for us?'

Which was why, in the snowy early spring of 1941, I sat correcting proofs of *Modern Reading 1* by lamplight in a damp bedroom of a cottage in the little village of Southoe, in Huntingdonshire. My first published story and our first child were due out at the same time.

Looking through these journals, my initial surprise is of coming across something I didn't know I knew or finding curious gaps. I had not written a word about my son's birth at

Paxton Park. Yet I had noted meticulously the couple on whom I was billetted – all mothers-to-be were evacuated for about six weeks – the village dialect, the frozen cabbage fields. I had noted my unease about Reginald in the air raids, doing his fire-watching stint on the rooftops of Victoria Street, for just before I left, the firebomb raids on the City had destroyed eight Wren churches and badly damaged the Guildhall.

Yet out of this time came 'Snowstorm' (originally titled 'The Hard and the Human' and published in Woodrow Wyatt's *English Story: 4th Series* (1943)) as well as 'Woman about the House'. Robert Frost was right when he noted: 'The impressions most useful to my purpose seem always to be those I was unaware of and so made no note of at the time.'

Back in London the raids were still heavy. People came up from the East End to find deep shelters. We saw them queueing up for places outside Dickins & Jones in late afternoons. Unforgettable times. Sitting in trains, we were wafted through the sound-proof underworld of the Tube, passing Henry Moore bodies swaddled in old blankets, pressed up against the curved walls. Outside the train, on the platforms, the noise reverberated from hollow spaces like the din in a swimming pool.

We did not believe in safety in numbers and avoided deep shelters after a tricky episode in Holborn. If we stayed in our room we put the baby in his carry-cot under the table and sat well back from the bandaged windows. I would wind up a little musical box I had bought in Munich before the war on a school visit, and tuck it in beside him so that he could listen to the fragile Berceuse rather than the whistle of bombs and the labouring throb of seeking planes. '*Gute Abend, gute Nacht* . . . ' but what did language matter? Music knows no frontiers.

We believed that if you accepted the fact that you might die, you felt quite safe, almost liberated. 'Firstborn', in *Modern Reading 3* belongs to this period. A little later came 'Lullaby', which attracted horrified letters from some readers.

Mass Observation gave the number of bombs dropped on London in 1940/41 as 18,800 tons.

* * *

We moved across London to a small mews cottage off the Adelaide Road in Swiss Cottage (since demolished to make way for a swimming pool and library). There we met James Hanley about to return to his home in Wales and anxious for us to follow. Within weeks a telegram arrived: 'Eureka. Found cottage. Nine fruit trees. Come immediately.' We decided to take the plunge.

Gelli was a traditional black and white Montgomeryshire cottage, two up, two down, with a boilerhouse attached. We had three-quarters of an acre of land, an outside privy in which the previous owner had shot himself, no electricity, and a pump outside the front door. We had apple, plum and damson trees and rich soil in which to grow vegetables. It cost 17/6 furnished (the same price as our first Bayswater bed-sit). On our arrival we found the table set with bread, butter, eggs, milk, cheese, and a kettle steaming on the fire in the range. After the privations of London we were overcome by this neighbourly welcome. Up our lane were only four cottages, and from every one of the couples who lived in them we learned something; the fine art of bastard trenching, the necessity of keeping one's glass chimney for the oil lamp clean, not to hang out washing on a Sunday, how to prime a reluctant pump. Lawrence (our son, now walking) soon was toddling over to Mrs Grindley for jam butties. Country life suited us.

One year we picked eighty pounds of damsons and twenty of plums: that night I remember the branches, freed of their burden of fruit, dancing their shadows across the ceiling and walls of our bedroom, cast by the light of a full moon. We sent most of the fruit to market and bottled the rest. We grew enormous leeks and marrows, taking the tip of our expert opposite to plant marigolds by them, to encourage pollination by bees. We grew beans and peas and potatoes, and pansies the size of coffee saucers. When they turned their faces to the sun they all looked like Hitler, with a small black moustaches.

The following year I had another child, and that winter saw snow and frost that froze the pump and also the bucket in which the baby's nappies were soaking. Nappies in aspic.

Looking back, I marvel at the sheer energy, both mental and physical, one can expend when young. From the tiny boilerhouse, Reginald not only founded and co-edited half a dozen magazines, wrote letters of encouragement to would-be contributors, juggled with publishers and agents and paper quotas and tried to get the magazines out on time and his writers paid, but also wrote his second novel *The Listening World* (published in America and England) and got together a volume of his own short stories.

My daughter was born on D-Day. At the Welshpool hospital the radio was going full tilt from dawn onwards. Reginald cycled nine miles each evening to see us, bringing more proofs to correct. I had finished a novella, *The Story of Stanley Brent*, just in time.

I had set myself the goal of producing two children and two novels before I reached twenty-five. I had my children and a novella, but the long novel needed considerable revision. My journal at that time is full of self-castigation. 'I am lazy, disorganised, my mind full of trivia . . .' 'I feel that in the future I shall pay for all these wasted half-hours, idle afternoons. Some sort of hated occupation will be forced on me, leaving me no time to think or feel or expand . . .' One or two gloomy stories written at this time echo that theme of self-punishment, but I have not included them in this collection.

What a mysterious alchemy writing is! We must be observant yet detached and always alert. I remember sitting opposite a woman on a darkened train from Paddington after a London visit, who told me she had left her flat and moved into a guesthouse near the coast; she liked the company. When I got home I sat down and wrote 'Tell It to a Stranger'.

* * *

On New Year's Day 1946 we moved into Glanbrogan Hall, a 300-year-old house set among fields. It had beautiful oak floors, five attics: one closed, one smelling of apples. From time to time footsteps could be heard in these empty rooms. Two of the bedrooms had powder-closets (for wigs), and a decorated Victorian lavatory was raised on a dais in the bathroom. The children had a playroom, we had a study. We were glad of the extra space and hot and cold running water, but still had to rely on oil-lamps. A traditional kitchen garden was enclosed by mellow brick walls but was full of nettles and ground elder. The stables housed – for a time – a pony and trap lent us by a neighbour, and when we heard the whistle of the afternoon train we would harness up Beauty and drive in to fetch the children from school. She knew we were tyros and was up to every trick in a pony's trade.

My mother sent furniture from London by Carter Paterson and it arrived on the dot of three o'clock as promised.

All this for 30/- a week.

In the surrounding fields Italian and German prisoners of war dug ditches and came to the house to sell their home made toys or cigarette lighters.

The bitter winter of 1947 taxed all our newly-won country skills. We were snowed up from January to March, having to forage for wood (there was no coal) with a home-made sledge, and dig our way with help to the village through lanes hedge-high with snow. Up in the hills farmers shot their starving cattle, and one farmer shot himself. The ground was too hard to bury him, so he was kept on ice until the thaw.

When school reopened, in spite of the floods, a Spring Eisteddfod was organised and our two, who now spoke Welsh, were awarded red ribbons for recitation and singing. These were deeply fulfilling and happy years, although there were ominous signs that the era of wartime anthologies was coming to an end. By 1950, when we returned to London, booksellers had swept them off their shelves. Naturally enough, peacetime called for a different reading diet.

But we had both had our novels and stories published over here and in the States, and I was particularly pleased to have had a poetry anthology on old age (always a bit of an obsession with me) called 'Man Goeth To His Long Home,' on the new Third Programme. Life would have been bleak indeed without the BBC. Our bakelite Philco wireless set was a lifeline. Plays, poetry, music, comedy, to keep one sane.

We were lucky to have been accepted into the rural community, on all levels. Like Alice, we were able to step effortlessly from square to square in this chessboard of social divides. Reginald started a Sports club, to assuage his passion for cricket. He learned the skill of scything at hay harvest, working alongside the POWs, for help was always needed. I joined the WI. We were good friends with our local landowners: maybe because we were still 'outsiders' or in modern parlance 'incomers'. We were also writers, and writers are classless. I wrote 'To Tea with the Colonel' and 'Subject for a Sermon' to try to pin down what I saw going on around us.

All the stories in this volume made their debut in the Hourglass Library in 1947, the blizzard year, with the exception of 'The Prisoner', which was written a year later. This series of selected short stories by twelve individual writers was edited by Reginald and beautifully produced in Dublin by Maurice Fridberg, because of the paper shortage. Re-reading these stories today, in their charming new clothes, I find faults that a young writer seemingly cannot avoid in the prentice years. I have made a few revisions to the text, but overall they stand or fall as they were written, as indeed they should.

Elizabeth Berridge
London, 2000

If you have enjoyed this Persephone book why not telephone or write to us for a free copy of the Persephone Catalogue and the current Persephone Biannually? All Persephone books ordered from us cost £10 or three for £27 plus £2 postage per book.

PERSEPHONE BOOKS LTD
59 Lamb's Conduit Street
London WC1N 3NB

Telephone: 020 7242 9292
sales@persephonebooks.co.uk
www.persephonebooks.co.uk

Persephone Books publishes forgotten fiction and
non-fiction by unjustly neglected authors. The following
titles are available: